D0909623

DISCARDED

BRODIE

BRODIE

MCKENDREE LONG

FIVE STAR
A part of Gale, Cengage Learning

GALE
CENGAGE Learning·

Farmington Hills, Mich • San Francisco • New York • Waterville, Maine
Meriden, Conn • Mason, Ohio • Chicago

GALE
CENGAGE Learning®

Copyright © 2017 by McKendree Long
Five Star™ Publishing, a part of Cengage Learning, Inc.

LIBRARY OF CONGRESS CATALOGING-IN-PUBLICATION DATA

Names: Long, McKendree R., author.
Title: Brodie / McKendree Long.
Description: First Edition. | Waterville, Maine : Five Star Publishing, a part of Cengage Learning, Inc., 2017.
Identifiers: LCCN 2016037332 (print) | LCCN 2016048370 (ebook) | ISBN 9781432833060 (hardback) | ISBN 1432833065 (hardcover) | ISBN 9781432833039 (ebook) | ISBN 1432833030 (ebook) | ISBN 9781432836849 (ebook) | ISBN 1432836846 (ebook)
Subjects: | BISAC: FICTION / Action & Adventure. | FICTION / Westerns. | GSAFD: Western stories.
Classification: LCC PS3612.O499 B76 2017 (print) | LCC PS3612.O499 (ebook) | DDC 813/.6—dc23
LC record available at https://lccn.loc.gov/2016037332

First Edition. First Printing: February 2017
Find us on Facebook– https://www.facebook.com/FiveStarCengage
Visit our website– http://www.gale.cengage.com/fivestar/
Contact Five Star™ Publishing at FiveStar@cengage.com

Printed in the United States of America
1 2 3 4 5 6 7 21 20 19 18 17

BRODIE

CHAPTER ONE

"Daddy. Daddy, wake up. Got to go."

Normally that would have woke me, even without the shaking. I didn't have any children. He was talking to me, though, and I knew who he was.

"Get up, Daddy. Get up. Got to go." Cracked-Head Billy was the only son of Cross-Eyed Lil, probably the friendliest working woman in Sweetwater. He was maybe thirteen in years, but he was about three bricks short of a load. Word was he'd been kicked in the head by a jack. Called every man he met "Daddy," and many of them could have been, but not me. I was maybe ten when Billy was born.

I said, "Billy, go ask your momma to put on some coffee."

"Can't," he said. "Got to go. Come on."

I started to drift off again, but the clicks of a pistol being cocked brought me up from the depths. I sat right up. Billy was pushing my Colt at me, butt first.

"Judas Priest, Billy, you don't play with my guns. Now, get your momma going on that coffee." I was right snappish.

"Can't," he said. "Momma's dead."

Something about the way he said it gave me goosebumps. I took that pistol from him and followed him downstairs. I didn't decock that Colt, neither.

My girlfriend snored on. Some might have thought Godiva Jones was a sinner, working in a place like the Alley Cat Saloon, but she slept the sleep of the innocent and unafraid. Clear conscience, I suppose.

Nobody else was up yet. Rising at the crack of dawn is not common at most brothels.

Cross-Eyed Lil was on the floor in the kitchen. Even Billy couldn't have mistook her condition. She was face down in a pool of blood. I knelt to check her neck for a pulse, but my fingers went right into her throat. She was cut from ear to ear.

Billy sat on a stool, biting his thumb and bobbing his head up and down.

"Dead," he muttered. "Dead, dead. Like a chicken. Not good, not good."

That's when I noticed Billy had blood all over him, and his momma was still warm.

"Billy, you got to talk to me. Did you do this to your momma? Did you hurt her?"

"Nooo," he wailed. "Bad men. Bad, bad men." He pointed to the back door and I heard horses snorting and a jumble of voices.

I jerked the door open and found myself staring into the rising sun. Several strangers were mounting up. These weren't no farmers. They were hard cases.

As I shielded my eyes with my left hand, I saw a shotgun swinging toward me, and I dove back in as it went off. Almost made it too. One buckshot pellet took me in the thigh. I think it bounced off the jamb.

I heard them yelling and pounding off and away, and I got off one round as they turned the corner. I was pretty certain I hit one, but there must have been four or five of them and I didn't make any of them out. I'd have run out there, maybe tried another shot, but I was barefoot and that back lot was nothing but hardpan, rocks, and sandburrs. Tenderfoot? My middle name.

"You know them, Billy? Are they the ones?"

"Them," he said. "Him. Good bad man. Him." He nodded.

"You know any names?"

He frowned, then nodded. "Chico."

"Chico did this?"

Billy shook his head. "No. Good bad man. He hurt her."

Everything went to pieces about then, as the law and the girls from upstairs showed up at the same time.

You ain't ever heard such hollering and confusion. Town Marshal Sentell asked me a few questions then told me to go get dressed. "Might need you to do something for me," he said.

By the time I got on my boots, shirt, and gunbelt and come back downstairs, the marshal had got the girls calmed down some and started them cleaning up.

He steered me out back. "Brodie," he said, "don't nobody in there know a durn thing 'cept for little Billy and he can't tell me jack-squat."

"Nobody saw anything?"

"Nope. That bunch must've rid in about dawn, come in the back here, and got aholt of Lil. Boss Lady says Lil gave 'em one of the stashes where they had money hid. Or maybe Billy did, after they cut his ma."

"What you gonna do, Marshal?"

He maybe thought for a second or two, but Curly Jack Sentell wasn't so much of a thinking man as he was a fixer. Things come clear to him pretty fast, and he went right at a problem. He shrugged and said, "Soon as I load up, I'm going after them. Gonna try to kill 'em. Anything to keep you from going along?"

I kind of knew that was coming. I had spent four years riding with the Frontier Battalion of the Rangers, before being let go to nurse a busted leg several months back. Same durn leg I just got shot in. But mainly I was healthy and footloose and well armed, and needing a job. Still, maybe I should've begged off. Things wouldn't have got so messed up later.

9

"I can go. You gonna pay me?"

"Town will. One hour enough, Deputy Dent?"

I grinned. I was back on a payroll. "One hour is plenty. How we gonna know them?"

"Hellfire," he said, "We'll have to take little Billy, cracked head or not. He's the only one has seen 'em."

CHAPTER TWO

We were a fine and determined-looking posse as we rode out, if small in number. Weren't none of us small. The marshal hisself was over six foot, thick moustache, and wore a tall faded gray hat. The brim curled up on the sides from him tying his big purple kerchief under his chin and over the top to keep it on when that Panhandle wind tried to carry us all away. He was partial to clean white shirts under his dark vest, and his striped pants tucked into tall boots made him look even bigger. I think he took such pains in his dress to offset the fact that he was totally bald on top.

I heard he lost his hair young and had got used to his nickname, but I still felt nervous calling him Curly. I was a hand shorter than him and lean like he was. I liked a red bib shirt and blue checkered pants, tucked in like him, with a tan canvas vest and straw hat. I thought I looked right sharp, and Godiva Jones had agreed as she kissed me farewell.

Little Billy was scrawny, but only two hands shorter than me. He looked like a farm boy, in his brogans, oversized gray shirt, and overalls. Flat-brimmed gray hat. Didn't even have a gun.

As we headed out of Sweetwater, the marshal said, "We need to get the boy some boots."

I laughed and said, "Good luck with that." Weren't no stores where we was headed.

The marshal give me this grim look. "We'll find some. A scarf too."

We couldn't ride hard after them like we might have if we'd had a bunch of men. Their tracks showed there was five of them, or maybe four and a packhorse. It wasn't but me and the marshal chasing them. We were pulling a packhorse, and Billy was riding with us, so we had to be kind of deliberate.

Still, Curly Jack Sentell wasn't what most folks would call a deliberate kind of a person, not if they thought deliberate and slow was the same. He'd rode with the Third Texas in the war, had been a Minuteman or a Texas Ranger for ten years after that, and took this marshal job three years back. From what I'd heard, there wasn't anybody you'd rather hit the trail with.

"You got a plan, Marshal?"

"I do," he said. "I thought I done told you. I plan to kill 'em. Every durn one."

"You did say that. How you see that happening, with them five against us two?"

"Do we catch 'em in the open out on these plains, I'll kill some of 'em with Sally Ann. Maybe all of 'em."

Everybody in Sweetwater knew who Sally Ann was. She was his .45-75 Winchester rifle, model of 1876, and it was near twice as powerful as the '66 and '73 Winchesters most of us carried. He was a famous long-shooter with it.

"I won't be much help if you take 'em on at long range."

"I'll knock down their horses, pin 'em down, and let you work in close," he said. "More likely though, we spot their fire one night, get up close, and blister them."

We rode west steady for several days. We could tell they was angling for Tascosa, a Mex sheep-ranching sort of village on the Canadian River.

Little Billy didn't say much, but he rode pretty good for somebody who'd never been on a ranch or farm. Heck, he grew up in various bawdy houses.

"When did you learn to ride, Billy? You're right fair at it," I said.

He nodded at the marshal and said, "Him."

Curly Jack said, "Lil was sort of my woman. Kinda like you and Godiva, only not so open. Billy ain't mine, but I taught him what I could. He's good with horses. It's how I got him the job in the stables."

"Lord, Marshal, I didn't have no idea."

"She had just left my room when they kilt her. I shoulda walked her to the Alley Cat, but she didn't want folks to know about us. Feared it would hurt her business. They must of followed her in."

"And you don't mean to take no prisoners."

"Not one. Not a single damn one."

"Yes," said Billy. "All bad."

"Another thing you seem to be confused on," Sentell said, "Billy ain't stupid. His thoughts get scrambled when he tries to say 'em is all."

Five or eight miles shy of Tascosa the gang turned north toward the river. We pulled up.

"They're probably gonna camp along the river. Ain't but an hour of light left. We'll go up slow, park Billy and the horses somewheres, and go on afoot. You got any more guns?"

I could see he thought I was barely ready for a fight, only showing two guns. I wore a cut-down '72 Colt as company to my Yellowboy, as they both used forty-four Henry Flats. Him, on the other hand, he wore a long-barrel forty-five Colt and had two Schofields in saddle holsters, along with that big-ass Winchester.

"I got a little Police Model in my saddle bag," I said, thinking, *I got three to your four, Mister Smart Mouth. Not too bad.*

"Pissant thirty-eight," he snorted. "Give it to Billy when we stop. And give him some extry cartridges. You can stick one of my Schofields in your belt when we go in."

We spotted a campfire a little after nightfall, but Marshal Sentell decided we'd pull back and wait 'til dawn.

"I thought you was hot to go in amongst 'em," I said. I don't know why I said it. Maybe I was feeling cocky since I knew then we were going to wait. And I guess I was still smarting a little over him acting like I didn't have enough firepower for a real Texas Ranger.

He give me this look. Sort of made my balls draw up in me. Then he smiled.

"I know you're as bold as a hungry coyote," he said, "but it come to me that maybe that there fire might belong to some Mex sheepherders. We could sneak up close and take a look, but I don't know how to tell a sleeping Mex from a sleeping bandito. We could ask 'em, I guess, but I thought we'd get ourselves down into one of these dry creek beds, have us a little fire and food and sleep, and get up close to 'em before daylight. If they's our folks, we'll see and take 'em over their coffee."

Feeling foolish as all hell, I said, "Sounds good, Marshal. I like it."

He was deadly quiet for a moment, and then he said, "Well, good."

We did what he said, and it almost worked. What happened was that something startled their horses, probably a dang armadillo, and woke 'em all up as we were starting to sneak over to their camp. Time we got close, we heard 'em ride off across the river toward Tascosa.

We turned to make that long walk back to where we'd left Billy and the horses. I even cussed some, but then Sentell looked back and perked up.

"Hold on, Deputy," he whispered. "They's still somebody in that camp. See that?"

I did. In that gray dawn, somebody walked between us and the embers of their fire. And then a horse whinnied. We turned back and moved in closer.

Whoever it was wasn't no Mex shepherd. He started singing, and he was Irish or I'll kiss your butt on Sunday. Marshal Sentell looked at me and nodded, real serious-like.

By now it was nearing daylight, and the rest of the gang was long gone. Sentell whispered, "I'll kill his horse. You shoot him, but don't kill him if you can help it."

Next thing you know, he fired. Ka-blam!

That bandit's Appaloosa went down like it was sledgehammered. The bandit looked at the horse, then faced us, and I fired. I hit him, but a Henry slug ain't like a buffalo round. He bounced right back up and got off two shots from his belt pistol.

Then Sentell shot him. He went ass over tea kettle. We jogged on up there. He was still alive, but was gasping. Turns out I'd hit him in the leg, and it was the same leg I'd shot him in back in town. That's why they'd left him in camp.

Sentell's three-hundred-fifty grain slug had caught that songbird in the right shoulder and near took off his arm.

"I don't know as I care to help you," Sentell said, "but ain't neither one of us even gonna try, unless you talk. You mark me?"

The man was wiry and red-headed, and his eyes were near closed with pain. He said, "I'm shot to pieces. What else you gonna do to me?" He had some grit.

Sentell got squinty-eyed. "You are sitting on your coffin and playing with the lid, Mick. You kilt a woman."

The bandit's head drooped. "I know, I know. I didn't want that. Sure, and what is it you want to know?"

"Who you ride with? Where they heading now?"

The man groaned. "Preacher Vance is the boss. They gone to try and snatch some Mex women. They left me 'cause I'se shot, but I'se supposed to double back and meet 'em on the way back to Sweetwater. Preacher figures everybody will be out looking for us, and not looking for us to come back. Said we'll duck in, grab some women, and head for New Mexico. Sell 'em at the silver mines, or on down into Mexico. Maybe to the Apaches."

I said, "Who killed the woman?"

"Her? Hell, Preacher did, to make the dimwit give us the money. I wanted to keep her, but Preacher said she weren't nothing but a vile whore. And of course she bit him. There was that too. You gonna try and patch me up now?"

Marshal Sentell said, "Not exactly. See, she wasn't no vile whore. She was my woman." He drew his Colt and shot the man in the forehead. Just like that. Took off the back of his head, of course, and knocked him flat where he was sitting.

I rubbed my aching leg. "If I was him, I don't think I'd of said that. Leastways, he don't need no patching now, although I might."

The marshal turned to me. "Take his boots. His scarf is ruint. I think we needs to grab our horses and get into Tascosa. All them sheep there, ought to be someone can look at your leg."

As I limped back to our camp I said, "I'm truly sorry about Lil." I didn't know what else to say. I surely didn't want to say too much and have him thinking I'd spent time with her.

He said, "She deserved better. She didn't have no rough edges."

CHAPTER THREE

Billy was awake and alert when we slogged into camp. "Kill him?" he asked.

Curly took off his hat and rubbed his bald head. "I ain't sure what you mean, Billy. We kilt one, but he said he weren't the one as kilt your mama. Said somebody called Preacher did that."

Billy got all jumpy. "Yes! Yes! Preacher man. Good bad man!"

"Well, dang, Curly, that's what he means. A good man gone bad."

"Yeah, I follow him now. No, Billy, he had done left. We're gonna try to catch him now. Problem is we still don't know how he looks, and won't, neither, until you points him out to us. Pull on these boots and get saddled up."

Billy held up a finger like to say, "Wait," and ran to his gear. He pulled some paper and a pencil from his saddle bags, squatted down, and whipped out a picture of this durn bandit leader in less time than it took me to figure out what he was up to.

"Him. Him," he said, and it was good too. Flat-brim hat, frock coat, one of them preacher shirts, all black except for a white tab right at his Adam's apple. Dark bushy hair and mustache, mean eyes. Big nose. Hell, I could have picked him out on a crowded street.

"Good Lord, Billy, how'd you do that? I ain't ever seen such a thing." I was amazed and it must have showed since Billy was grinning like a pig in a mud puddle.

The marshal took it and folded it into his coat. "Told you he weren't no dummy." Now we knew what our target looked like, but it didn't do us any good right away. Time we got to Tascosa the banditos had already come and gone. They'd shot up some Mex sheepherders, stole a mule and a wagon, and loaded two Mex women and one girl into it.

And one white woman. Her husband was working on the wounded Mex men, and he told us what had happened.

"I'm Rawley Byden," he said. "Me and my bride Emmalee came here from Michigan last year. Sold my farm there. Thought we'd try sheep ranching out here. Anyhow, me and most of the men and boys was out since midnight, trying to round up sheep that was scattered by some coyotes. I don't speak too much Mex, but these two, Pablo and Vasquez, they say four gringos rode in here at dawn. Shot them down and killed Pablo's boy. Took the women and my wagon and headed west."

"West," I said. "Not back toward Sweetwater?"

"West," he said and pointed. "They'll be easy to track. They took my mule, but Vasquez here will lend me his. I'm going after them soon as I patch up these two."

Curly Jack said, "Did one of 'em go by 'Preacher' by chance?"

"Lemme ask." Byden turned to the wounded men. *"Esta uno gringo el padre?"* He folded his hands like he was praying. Probably the only reason they understood him, as his Mex wasn't much better'n mine.

"Si! Si!" They both nodded. *"El padre. Un padre mal."*

We got that much. Curly Jack said, "He kilt my woman back in Sweetwater, Mister Byden. We're gonna run 'em down. You can travel with us if you can keep up."

"I'll keep up," Byden said. "My wife ain't showing yet, but she's been carrying maybe two or three months. You know I got to get her back, and before they cause her to lose that baby. We already lost one."

He was kind of old, maybe forty. He looked half lost himself and half mad as hell.

"You some kind of doctor?" I asked.

He shrugged. "I guess you could say some kind. I was a farrier in Custer's regiment in the war on account of I come from a farm. Knew something about taking care of animals, birthing and all. When our surgeon got sick they made me a medico, since I was sort of a horse doctor. And I see you got a limp. And blood on your britches."

And that was the first time he cut me. Made a "X" in my thigh with a white-hot knife, then plucked out that flattened buckshot and some fabric to boot. Good thing I stumbled upon him, I suppose, though I wasn't sure of it right then.

"Already festering," he said as he took that stick out of my mouth. After I quit cussing, he poured something on the cut that made me cuss some more, then slapped a bandage on it. "You'll have a nice scar there. Sign of the Cross, right on your thigh."

"Well, Hot Dang," I snorted. "Maybe this Preacher Vance will plumb envy me."

Next time he cut me was a lot later on, and a whole different affair. I'm glad I didn't know that was coming and have it to look forward to. Horses and sheep might of tolerated his doctoring but I thought he was rough as a cob.

As it was, though, an hour later we rode west, more or less friends. The village blacksmith, another white man name of Kendall, had give Billy a big old blue kerchief.

We crossed back over and followed the south bank of the Canadian the rest of that day and never saw our quarry. Even when it got dark we couldn't see any sign of a fire up ahead of us.

"These boys lied to that Irishman they left in their camp," said Curly as we settled into a dry gully to set up camp. "They is headed straight for Santa Fe. Must of wanted him to double back and lead us astray."

"I'm worried we can't make out their fire," I said. "Either they're in a cold camp or they're moving faster than I figured."

Curly Jack said, "They ain't tracking nobody and they ain't watching ever which way for a durn ambush, like we got to. Of course they're moving faster."

"I don't see why we're stopping," Byden said. "We ain't tired. I'm telling you, we need to catch 'em before they hurt my wife."

"Well, you go right on, Mister Byden. You got that Spencer and that old Remington cap and ball. Canteen and some jerky, you'll be fine." Curly Jack dropped his saddle on the ground. "Less'n you step in a chuck hole in the dark, or stumble into 'em, maybe get your ass shot off. Deputy Dent works for me, so me and him and Billy are gonna get some food and shut-eye."

Byden hadn't dismounted. "You'd sing a different tune if they had your woman. Maybe you're scared of the dark?"

"They done kilt my woman, and all I'm scared of is losing my mount out here, and then losing them. You might oughta calm down and climb down. That's an almighty high horse you're on right now, and I ain't talking about your mule."

Byden snorted, yanked that mule around, and rode off in the dark. The rest of us had a delicious dinner made up of a cold can of stewed tomatoes, jerky, and stale water, and then went to sleep.

Three hours later the gunfire woke us up.

Curly said, "Well, at least he didn't step in no hole. Horse droppings, maybe."

"We going over there? It sounds to be over two miles, maybe."

"It could be a sight further than that, out on these plains.

Naw. No point in us stumbling into them in the dark. It ain't midnight yet, and they're all stirred up. Hell, they're liable to load up and move, and Byden's dead or he ain't. Either way, he'll keep 'til morning. You and Billy best get some more rest. We got more'n five hours afore dawn."

I said, "You ain't sleeping?"

"I'll watch for an hour or two, make sure Byden don't lead 'em right back here. I'll wake one of y'all up then and we'll do shift watches 'til daybreak. Then we'll go pick up the pieces. Get some sleep. They's a long way off." Sleep. Right. Good luck with that.

CHAPTER FOUR

Curly wouldn't let us start a fire for coffee, so we were moving soon as we could see. Couple of miles west and Byden hailed us. He was afoot, but didn't look to be hurt.

Curly shouted, "Where are they?"

"Gone," Byden yelled back. He pointed west. "That way. Maybe five hours ago."

Curly turned to me. "He don't have no idea where they are. You circle him, ride out and find their camp, see is they really running again. Me and Billy will pick up Byden, follow on slow."

I said, "All right," and started away.

"Brodie," he said. "They might not be running. Don't ride into no ambush. Soon as you make out they're really on the run, come on back. But if they're laying for you, I'll hear it and come on fast."

I headed out at a good pace. Thing about that area was that there weren't a lot of places to hide a wagon and a bunch of horses, so as to set up an ambush.

Still, there were enough creeks and washes and patches of trees to keep me awake. Plenty of room to swing wide of them, though, to come in from behind and watch for wagon tracks.

That was how I found their trail, several hours out. Far side of a creek with a small stand of trees. I tracked them west a couple more miles, then turned back. They had camped on that creek and had a fire. I guess the trees and the fact they was in a gully kept us from seeing the glow.

Looked to me like Byden had rid almost right up on them before somebody heard him and opened up. I found a blood trail going back east and maybe a hundred fifty paces on that way was Byden's borrowed mule.

He was in a ditch and was dead, shot full of holes. Byden must of hit the ground running and then kept on going. I found his Spencer rifle in the weeds near the mule, then headed back to look for Curly.

They had come on pretty good, considering Byden was riding double with Billy. Wasn't much more than a hour before we hooked up.

"Looking for this?" I handed Byden his Spencer. "It was near your friend's mule. The dead one."

Byden didn't smile. "Thanks. I lost it when the mule went down. I got off two quick shots when I stumbled on 'em. Before the mule was hit and bolted, I mean."

Curly said, "Probably why they didn't follow you. Knew they was up against a repeater. Didn't figure you'd dropped it. Anyways, let's hope you didn't hit no women. Did you think on that?"

Byden hung his head and said, "Not really. I mean, I wasn't thinking at all. They startled the hell out of me, and I was just shooting back. You pick up my canteen, by chance?"

I said, "I saw it. Two holes in it, look to be buckshot. You must be hit too."

"Scrape on his side, another along his leg," Curly kind of laughed. "His clothes is full of holes. No question but he used up all his luck."

"Watch for lightning," Billy said, grinning.

"That'll be your worry, boy," Curly said. "You got to ride with him. Let's move. They been rolling since midnight, got near a half day's lead on us."

"All right," I said. "We can pick up Byden's bedroll off that mule as we pass their camp, and see did I miss anything else. I did pick up two fifty-seventy casings and one fifty-ninety, left near their fire."

"That ain't good," said Curly.

"What do you mean?" asked Byden.

"They got at least two buffalo guns," Curly said. "Long shooters. We can't go hot after 'em, even if we wasn't pulling a packhorse. And got some dumbass riding double because he don't listen."

I said, "Means we might as well stick together. No point in me and the marshal leaving you two with the packhorse, and us taking off fast."

Byden said, "I'm sorry, I really am."

Billy nodded his head and Curly said, "Yes. Yes you are."

I felt kind of sorry for Byden right then, missing his wife and all, but after all he had slowed us down and made things worse. Had to wonder whose durn side he was on, and it wasn't like those banditos needed more help.

Two days into New Mexico territory, we spotted smoke ahead and north across the Canadian River. We followed the wagon tracks right up to the crossing.

It was a small ranch. Good-sized sod house with some other wood outbuildings, maybe a barn and stable. It was hard to tell exactly as one was burning and the other was smoldering.

Rawley Byden said, "I think that's my wagon, out back of the soddy. I had a red board in the left side like that, where I patched it."

Curly was glassing the spread, so I pulled my scope too.

"Brodie, you spy any horses?"

"Nary a one, Marshal. You figure that gang has come and gone?"

"I do. I hope ain't everybody dead here. Let's walk up slow."

Somebody hailed us from the soddy about then as we were making our way uphill from the river.

"Who are you, and what is it you come for?" Sounded like a boy.

Curly yelled back. "Don't shoot. I'm the law out of Sweetwater, Texas. We're after a gang of bandits that prob'ly come in here with that wagon in back."

"You missed 'em. Killed poor Jim, winged Mama. Took our horses and mules and set our sheds afire, but we run 'em off."

"Your stable might live, but I believe your barn is done for. Can we come up? We got a man who knows something about doctoring."

The soddy door opened and a boy stepped out. Looked to be maybe fifteen.

"Y'all come on up. Your man can look at my mama. She's shot up some. Other ones can maybe help me with that fire."

There wasn't a single thing we could do with that fire, except watch that barn crumple into history.

The woman had half her left ear shot off plus a finger gone. Another finger was busted and gouged pretty good alongside the missing one. She also had a buckshot pellet in her boney butt.

Byden went to work on her while we listened to her son unload like a busted dam.

"They caught Mama and Jim down toward the river. Jim's Mama's man. I mean, he was. My daddy died of fever a good while back. Mama called me in from the barn and we run, but they hit her with some buckshot as she shooed me in the door. Missed me entire."

"Not entire," I said. "You got a neat cut along your hairline, over your ear. Right side."

He touched his head and stared at the blood on his fingers for a second.

"Well, I be durned. Didn't even notice. Anyways, we had Jim's shotgun and Daddy's old Smith carbine, which I used in the main. Mama reloaded them Injia-rubber cartridges for me, and she watched behind me, whichever winder I was at. She had Daddy's Richards Colt. She was shooting it out that back winder right there, chasing them away from their wagon, when they near shot her hand off."

"Yes, hell, they did," she said from face-down on the table where Byden was cutting that little lead pill out of her butt.

I glanced back at that god-awful sight. I turned back to the boy pretty quick, even though she kept talking.

"Didn't hurt the pistol much. I's able to pick it up left-handed and empty it at them sonsabitches, but reloading weren't no simple damn task, I can tell you."

Her voice was as raspy as she was salty, and she told us why.

" 'Bout lost my voice, screaming at 'em the whole time. 'Get away from us, you bastards,' I said. 'Leave us alone, you filthy damn dogs. I'll kill you.' I let 'em know how I felt. I'da throwed rocks and plates at 'em if I'da run outta bullets. Sonsabitches."

Salty. She was as salty as I ever seen. I'm guessing the boy's daddy rescued her from a place like the Alley Cat Saloon. Or maybe he rescued the whorehouse from her.

"You done good, Mama. You purely did." The boy had caught his breath. "And we run 'em off. When they shot Mama's hand, I took the shotgun and run out and around the side. They had cut the wagon mules a-loose and chased 'em down past the barn. I surprised 'em, got off a couple of blasts. Knocked one down and caused one to scream. Mighta been the same one I knocked down."

He took a breath. I had begun to worry he might pass out.

"O'course, coulda been Mama as knocked him down. She

opened that winder on the barn side and was cussing and shooting left-handed. We drove 'em down past the stables, but they'd already took our mules and horses. 'Cept for one, o'course. My big brother Willy was off on it, rounding up some cattle. . . ."

"Which is why he wont here to help us," the woman broke in. "We'da had him here, they might not of took such advantage of us. Willy's a damn sight, tougher than this one."

Curly Jack said, "I don't see how nobody could have done no better than this boy. No way do I see it."

"Yeah," she cackled, "I guess he done all right."

The boy beamed, nodded, and started again. Sweet Jesus.

"Then they torched the barn and horse shed, and run off. Me and Mama splashed water from the horse trough on the shed, put it out, but we saw we couldn't do nothing for the barn. 'Cept rebuild it, I guess. We had barely drug poor Jim's body up from where they shot him, and put him in here when we saw you working your way upriver from the other side. That's Jim, there in the corner."

I said, "Unh-huh." Who the heck else would he be?

"You both done good," the marshal said. "So, how long since they left?"

"Four hours, maybe more. Took us a while afore we crept out, then we was slow fighting that fire, what with Mama's bad hand. And we seen y'all coming a long ways off, and braced up for another fight."

Chapter Five

"Marshal, I don't want to leave my wagon here, whenever we press on."

We were bedding down in and under that very wagon. By the time Byden finished his patchwork on the woman of the house and we buried her man, it was growing dark. They had fed us some beef and beans, and the marshal decided to lay over.

Curly Jack stared at Byden for a few seconds and then said, "Why?"

Byden seemed startled that the marshal didn't bite his head off and say no right off. Fact is, I was surprised myself. Still, Byden got right to it.

"We can take everything off the packhorse and put it in the wagon, and him and Billy's horse can pull it. Me and Billy will drive the wagon. I don't see how it'll be no slower than us riding double. Main thing, though, is when we catch 'em, we might need it for the trip home. My wife ought'n to be riding no horse, and you know that's what they done here."

"Put the women prisoners on horses and mules, you mean?" I had thought that for a bit, but was glad for the chance to see what Curly thought.

"It's exactly what they done," said Curly. "Now they'll pull away, whichever we decide, wagon or no."

"So it's all right then? We can take it?"

I swear he was about to jump up and sing hallelujah. I think he was more worried about losing that wagon than ought else.

"Yeah, we'll take it. Could be we wind up fighting this Preacher and his boys, and anybody could get shot, us or the women. Might need the wagon to haul wounded. Now get to sleep. We got to roll early to halfway sort of keep up with 'em."

I said, "One more thing, Marshal. We know what Preacher looks like now. Don't really need Billy no more. You and me could ride hard, maybe catch up to 'em. Let Mister Byden and Billy follow along slow."

Curly shook his head. "I done thought on that. Billy don't know jack-shit about tracking, and this horse doctor knows less. No, I reckon we'll stick together."

I could see he was right. I sure didn't want Billy getting lost and perishing out in the wilds somewhere. Had to be awful what he'd already gone through. I'd tried to get him to talk some on it, on the trail to here. All he'd do was frown and shake his head and say, "Cain't."

He'd only got to know his momma about as much as I did mine. I was born over in Fort Bend county about six years before the war. Daddy went to ride with the Eighth Texas Cavalry, alongside most of the men from around there.

He died at Franklin, Tennessee, whether from sickness or bullets we never knew. Momma died of fever when I's about ten, about the time the fighting stopped. She never was lucky.

I had two sisters and a brother, all older than me. We was put with a family in Victoria. The man had rode with Daddy and lost an arm, but it was before Daddy died so he couldn't tell us nothing about Daddy's death. What he could do was work our butts to a frazzle.

He owned a hardware store and the stables, and ran a little cook shed and cantina for the stages that changed horses with us. It was a booming business, with folks around us on hard times, but he never paid none of us Dents a durn dime. I did learn horses and guns and cooking and leather there, and how to do without.

One night when I was about fourteen, my brother woke me up in the barn and said, "Let's go."

"Where to?"

"Most anywhere would do, but I was thinking Austin."

I said, "We ain't never been there." I was struggling to wake up.

"We ain't ever been nowhere, 'cept Houston. C'mon, get your ass up."

It hit me then why I was so groggy. It was pouring rain outside and I'd been sleeping like a dead man. I do love that sound.

"James, it's pouring down. We can't go nowhere." Much as I loved that sound, I only enjoyed it when I was inside.

"It's a frog strangler," he grinned. "Big storm building. We'll be long gone before they miss us, and won't be able to track us once they do. Grab your slicker and stick this in your belt."

He handed me a Smith and Wesson Number Two Army and a box of thirty-two-caliber rimfire cartridges.

"I done saddled your pony, got you a full canteen, and put jerky and corn dodgers in your saddle pockets. Roll up your blanket in that piece of canvas, and we'll make our departure."

James liked to use big words like *departure*.

"What about Sally and Lucy? They coming too?" I was pulling on my brogans.

"Oh, hell no, Brodie, our sisters will be gone and married before winter. I told Lucy we was heading toward the coast, so's she won't have to lie."

"So, lemme get this straight. We stealing guns and horses and tack?"

"And food and ammunition, and a little cash. Only it ain't theft. It's less than that one-armed bandit owes us, after four years of slave labor."

Turns out that storm was the August hurricane of 1869, and it came in at Matagorda Island. Me and James were listed as missing and feared dead. Seems they found a dead Appaloosa, looked like the one I stole, up in a tree at Indianola.

We made it to Austin fine. James joined the Texas Rangers there, and they hired me as helper to the camp cook. That didn't take, and they moved me pretty quick to helping with the remuda. Soon as they let me, I joined up too.

My trip down memory lane ended when Curly Jack kind of kicked me on the bottom of my feet. I sat right up and banged my head on the wagon axle.

"Let's get 'em moving," he said. He was rolling up the rope he'd circled our wagon with. Said it would keep snakes out. Scorpions too.

I shook my boots all the same. The marshal hadn't made no promises about tarantulas.

Come dawn we were several miles west of the old hag and her talkative son. The Canadian River turned north at that point, and the preacher's trail crossed back over and went on west.

So did we. We could see mountains straight ahead, but a long ways off.

"Those is the Sangre de Cristo mountains," Curly told us. "Maybe two days out. Las Vegas is on this side of 'em. Santa Fe is another day's ride the other side. You go south then up through Glorieta Pass."

"Sangre de Cristo," I said. "What does it mean?"

"Blood of Christ," Byden said. Could be his Mex was better'n mine after all.

"Bloody Hell would be better," said Curly. "They's been fighting with Indians around them mountains since the white man come, and with Mexs before that."

Little Billy shuddered and said "Blood."

Premonition, I guess.

CHAPTER SIX

We hit the Santa Fe Trail late the next day, maybe halfway between Las Vegas and the Glorieta Pass.

"Which way?" I asked Curly.

"I had a coin, I'd toss it to see. Ain't no way to trail 'em through all them tracks. They coulda gone either way."

"Well, make up your mind," said Byden. "We need to keep moving."

For somebody who sort of single-handed had slowed us down so much, he had long ago got on my nerves. That little crack tore it for me.

I said, "Bold talk for somebody who don't know his ass from a hole in the ground."

He went red-faced and reached for his Spencer in the wagon bed behind him. I drew, cocked, and covered him before he could pick it up. He froze when he heard my Colt click up. He might of lacked good sense, but he wasn't stupid.

"No fighting," said Billy.

"Don't shoot him, Brodie. I ain't sure Billy can handle the wagon by hisself." Curly watched, grinning. "What we'll do, Mister Racehorse Byden, is me and Deputy Dent will go left and scout out Santa Fe in the morning. You take your precious wagon and Billy and head north into Las Vegas. Can't be ten miles. You can't get lost."

"I didn't mean to get snappy. Wasn't no cause for it. What do we do if we find Preacher and his gang in town? I mean, he'll

33

know this wagon."

Curly frowned at me. "Shoot, Brodie, he's right. Put your pistol up and calm down. We'll see can we make Las Vegas by dark. Together."

As I reholstered, Billy said "Look," and pointed south.

I thought he wanted to study the pass, so I tossed him my scope.

He extended it, peered in and said, "Riders." He held up three fingers.

I said, "Gimme that," but Byden snatched it.

"My Lord," he said. "That's Kendall's wife."

Curly had his scope on them by then. "What about them two men? Give it back to Billy. Billy, is they some of the gang? Don't neither of 'em look like your picture of Preacher."

Billy looked again and said, "No. Not them." He closed the telescope and tossed it back to me, so's I finally got a peek.

"That looks like a squaw to me. How sure are you it's one of the prisoners?"

"Damn sure. That's Señora Terrazas, Kendall's wife. Sure as I'm sitting here."

Curly said, "That don't tally. How come she ain't Señor Terraza's wife?"

Byden said, "Terrazas died, and she took up with Kendall. He's our blacksmith."

"Well," said Curly, "If y'all is sure, then these two yahoos has probably run into Preacher and either bought or stole that Mex woman from him. She speak any American?"

"Nary bit," said Byden.

"Good. Don't want her to see us and let on she knows you. We'll head toward Las Vegas, slow-like, let 'em overtake us. Byden, you keep your face away from her 'til we get the drop on 'em. And get that Spencer up beside you 'stead of down in the bed."

I said, "I don't see why we don't go right at 'em."

"Brodie, we don't know but what these two found her running loose and is merely bringing her to town. Main thing is, if she is a prisoner, we don't want her recognizing Byden and starting to hoot and holler for help."

"What stops them from riding up close and backshooting us?"

"Now see, Deputy? Now you're thinking. That's a good thought. What we'll do is, once they's a hundred yards back, you and me will stop and wait for 'em. Pull off on the side, let Byden and Billy ride on slow. Soon as we cover 'em, Byden can turn back and question that woman."

I drew my Yellowboy and laid her across my pommel. Curly did the same with Sally Ann.

It took half an hour for them to close up. We backed off sideways and when they was twenty yards out Curly hailed them.

"How do?" he yelled. "You tell us how far to Las Vegas? We is inbound from Texas."

I heard him thumb his hammer back on that big Winchester while he was yelling, so I cocked my carbine too.

They were both lean and dirty, much like us. Both had Henry rifles and had them out. The taller one said, "Straight ahead. Can't be more'n an hour. Ride with us. We plan to stay the night there. See can we pick up a few pesos sharing this here señorita we bought over in Santa Fe."

Curly said, "Bought her, did you? Didn't realize you could still do that. This surely ain't Texas."

The shorter one laughed. "No, hell no, it ain't. Y'all can sample her first, if you got three dollar apiece."

"Five, if you want special treatment," said the tall one.

He leaned over to spit, and Curly swung Sally Ann to cover him. I got the drop on the other.

"I think what we'll do is take her off your hands," Curly said, then yelled at Byden, "Come on back!"

The tall one said, "The hell you say, Tex," and they both jerked their rifles toward us.

Curly's slug knocked the tall one right out of his saddle. My shot hit Shorty's Henry, knocked it away, but he yanked out a big Smith and Wesson and got off one round before I dropped him with my second shot. See, my horse danced a little to the music of those Winchesters.

I swung down, ran over, and put another round in each of them straight away. Shorty's foot was still in the left stirrup, and his horse dragged him off a little ways after I shot him, but he wasn't done. When his foot came loose he tried to stand so I dusted him again and he stayed down. Third time's a charm.

I checked the tall one and I had wasted a bullet on him. "You killed this one dead as a stone, Curly," I said as I stood and turned toward the marshal.

"Well, you was a bit slow with yourn," he said, then slid out of the saddle. His left side was covered with blood.

Bloody Hell is right, I thought.

CHAPTER SEVEN

Next few minutes was pure bedlam.

Byden come roaring up in the wagon, yanked the team to a halt, jumped down, and run to the Mex woman. She hopped down and hugged him and they commenced to shout gibberish at one another.

Billy slid over and put on the footbrake, then sprung down and run to me and Curly saying, "No, no!" He had that little Colt Police in his hand.

I took him by the shoulders and shook him. "Easy, boy. We're gonna take care of Curly. He ain't dead. You go see if that one that shot Curly is finished, then bring his horse back over here."

He looked wild for a second, then nodded and took off to check Shorty.

I yelled at Byden. "Y'all stop jabbering and come help me get Curly in the wagon."

Byden ran to us and started unbuttoning Curly's bib shirt and said, "Get me some water."

As I went to do that, I saw the Mex woman had turned the tall dead one over, unbuttoned his trousers, and had begun to saw away at his privates with his own knife.

"Hey!" I yelled, but I was interrupted by gunfire. I drew and spun to see Billy standing over Shorty, blasting him with that little Colt. He put all four balls in him. Between the gunsmoke and the dust coming off Shorty's clothes, I could barely make them out.

"I believe he's done now, Billy. Go get his pony."

I turned back in time to see the Mex woman stand up and shake the big one's bloody balls in his face. Like he could see it. She growled something in Mex at him and then flung his nuts into the bushes.

I said, "Good Lord, Señorita. I mean, Good Lord!"

She turned and gave me the sweetest smile and touched her chest. "Señora," she said. "Me. Señora Terrazas."

Byden yelled, "You two quit jawing and get over here. Bring the water. *Aqua,* dammit, *andale!*"

I handed him my canteen and squatted down beside him. "He out cold?" I said.

"Naw, he's awake, only got his eyes scrunched shut. Hurting pretty good, I suspect. It went through, bounced off his shoulder blade. May have busted it." He gave Curly a sip, then splashed water on the little blue hole.

Curly opened one eye and muttered, "Thankee."

"Bleeding has about stopped, and it never did spurt. Which is a good thing."

Curly said, "Durn sure is."

Byden nodded and continued, "Once we get him in the wagon, I'll have Señora Terrazas hold his kerchief over the holes, front and back. I hope there to be a real doctor in town. Let's lift him."

"Y'll help me up. I can walk. I ain't shot in the legs. Don't know how come I was to faint."

"It's called shock, Marshal, and it can take down the strongest men. Ain't no shame in it," Byden told him as we pulled him to his feet.

He was one tough old codger. "I been shot before and didn't pass out like no durn baby." He hobbled to the back of the wagon. "Get up in there, Brodie, and pull me up. And if it's all the same to you, I'd as soon y'all didn't say nothing to nobody about me fainting. I got a little light-headed is all."

At that moment his eyes rolled back and he went to his knees. I grabbed him to keep him from going down on his face.

"Unh-huh," I said. "Yeah. You're doing fine, ain't you? Y'all help me lift him in there and let's roll."

We got Curly and the Señora settled in the wagon bed with him laying on his right side and his head on Billy's saddle. I told Billy to ride there too, but he shook his head and hopped down.

We strung the three new mounts to the wagon, took in the stirrups on Curly's horse for Billy, and got moving.

I pushed five fresh cartridges into my carbine's gate and was pleased to see Billy reloading that little Colt I'd given him, but he couldn't hardly quit looking at Curly. Ever now and then he'd give me a quizzical look, but all I could do was say, "He'll be fine, Billy." Fact was, though, that I didn't have one clue in hell how Curly was.

It didn't help none that the Señora was chattering almost constant for the next half hour and then she only quit to wail and cry some.

I said, "Byden, what in the hell is she going on about? Does she think Curly is dying?"

"Naw," said Byden. "She says he's doing good. Not much new blood. What's wrong is, you know that little Mex girl they took? She's her daughter. Only fourteen years old, which is bad enough, but to top that off she's deef."

Billy said, "Deef?"

"She can't hardly hear jack-squat. Preacher and his boys already smacked her around some for not listening to 'em. They was gonna sell the girl to them two you killed back there, but Miz Terrazas raised so much sand they whacked her upside the head and got rid of her instead."

Curly muttered some cuss words and said, "You serious?"

Byden said, "I'm serious. Only reason she's still with us is I told her we're after the gang. If she had any sense of direction, she'd be off this wagon and hoofing it back the other way."

I said, "Good Lord."

"That's right," Byden said. "Another thing. You ain't gonna contain her long in this Las Vegas place we're heading to. Nor me. I don't care if it's some desert paradise."

Curly snorted. "It ain't."

I said, "Curly Jack, you doing all right there?"

He said, "Hell, I'm peachy keen. Morning sun is killing my eyes though."

Now, that particular answer about scared the mess out of me. See, it was near dark, and the sun had fell behind the Sangre de Cristo mountains some minutes earlier.

"Stroke that team, Mister Byden," I said. "Let's put a little push on. We needs to get the marshal outta this bright sunlight."

We got into the village of Las Vegas long after dark, and were steered to this church mission straight away.

Some priests come and swarmed over the marshal. Curly had begun to rave some so they gave him a stout drink of liquor, once they took off his shirt and saw he wasn't gutshot.

One of them, must have been the head man, was gray-haired and had a sharp, thin face, like a hawk. He said to leave Curly in their care. Said they run a kind of hospital, and him and a few others even spoke English.

I said, "I'd like to leave the boy with him. We're going after the men that killed his momma. Might be gone a while."

Before the priest could answer, Billy yanked my arm and said, "No." He said it right firm.

I started off to tell Billy why I wanted him to stay, but right then Señora Terrazas found out from one of them priests that we were in Las Vegas instead of Santa Fe, and she started in on me and Byden. I'm pretty glad I couldn't tell exactly what she was calling us even though her meaning was clear.

The priest calmed her by shouting at her, which appeared to scare the hell right out of her. Me and Rawley Byden told her we would all three head for Santa Fe at dawn.

Billy said, "Four."

I saw in his eyes that he was going, with or without us. I guess if I'd seen somebody kill my momma, I'd have been the same way.

I nodded. And about then durn if them priests didn't bring us soup and bread. Said they were Jesuits, whatever the heck that is. Sounded sort of Mexican, but said they's from Italy.

They gave Señora Terrazas a room and a rope cot. Me and Billy and Byden slept in the wagon, outside the mission walls.

Chapter Eight

We got off early next morning and pushed hard but it was still noon of the second day later before we come into Santa Fe. We parked Billy and the Señora and the wagon by the *zocalo,* told them not to go nowhere, and me and Byden started visiting the cantinas.

In the third one we went in, a drover spoke up right away.

"Shoot, y'all are looking for that preacher and his whores. They was here. Last I heard they'd took over a roadhouse down the Albuquerque road, maybe five miles south. They got one old fifty-cent Mex whore, but they also got a young'un and a white one that runs five dollar a pop."

I thought Byden was going to shoot the man right there.

"Bite your tongue, Mister Byden. I know you're eager as me, but we don't want to buy no pigs in a tote sack." I give him a wink and turned back to the drover. "Might be the ones we seek. Did you mark how many they was? We come a good ways to see can we buy some of their women."

"How many what? I mean, they's three men with the preacher. He's got three whores left. He done sold one or two. You buying for the railroad?"

I nodded, and Byden stormed out.

The drover laughed. "You can tell your friend there ain't no hurry. The old Mex woman ain't nothing special, and that preacher has got the other two priced so high that they ain't gonna sell anytime soon. He ain't even getting much rental action on 'em."

I caught Byden about a mile south of town.

I said, "You gonna go strolling in there, maybe get your woman killed in a crossfire?"

He slowed down. "What's your idea?"

"I think we play it sort of like we did back there. Act like we're there to sample the women, maybe buy them."

He said, "Buy them with what? I got no money. You got money?"

"Naw, I don't, neither, not enough. But I do have five dollars. And I got an extra pistol I took off them two we killed three days ago. If we can get your wife in a back room for a taste, we can slip her a gun and let her know we're working on it."

Byden looked at me funny and said, "Well, you'll have to let me have the money to do that."

"Jehosaphat Christmas, Byden, I ain't trying to slip in a poke with your wife. Of course, you do it. Maybe we don't even have to do all that. Maybe two of 'em is sleeping, or gone to eat or something, and we ain't outnumbered."

"What then?"

"Hell, Byden, we shoot 'em. Just do what I do."

"But what if all four of 'em is there? You thought about that?"

"Well, yes I have. We take a look at the women, say we like 'em but we need to go back into Santa Fe for the money. Say wasn't no way we was bringing gold coins into no possible ambush. Get two of 'em to go with us."

Byden got a shrewd look on his face.

"Yeah. That'll work. We'll say two of them got to stay in town with the rest of our gang as hostages until we come and pay for the women and bring 'em back to town. And once we get them away and get the drop on 'em, we can tie 'em up and go back and deal with the last two."

"We ain't tying nobody up, Byden. I'm gonna shoot both of 'em, first chance I get. You can help if you want. Then we're going back and kill the other two. We square on that?"

He nodded.

It almost worked that way.

We made one wrong stop at a small ranch, but the old Mex rancher steered us to the right place, half a mile on down the road, not much past a dry wash.

Byden went all tense as we rode up. He said, "There's five or six horses out back. What if they got customers? I'm telling you, Dent, I walk in there and some man is trying to root with my wife, I'm killing him first."

"Hush," I said. "Get ahold of yourself or you'll get us all killed. There ought to be at least seven mounts here. Could be some of 'em is gone. Durn sure ain't no extra horses. You wait outside so's your wife don't scream and give us away. I'll go in, act like I'm seeing if we's in the right place. Your wife don't know me, nor do any of the others. I'll let her know somehow you're with me, before I call you in."

Byden nodded. "Tell 'em Doctor Pudding Rawley is with you."

"Do what?"

"The Mex's all call me Doctor, and she calls me Pudding. The bandits ain't likely to know my first name, but they probably know she's Miz Byden by now. Yeah. Doctor Pudding Rawley."

"All right, Puddin'. But you make sure they's a round in that Spencer when you walk in. And your pistol ain't tied down."

I checked the chamber on my carbine, swung down, and went in fast.

It was clear I startled them all. Two men sat at a table with a jug between them. Partly hid behind a curtain were two women and a girl sitting on two wood beds.

Both men went slack-jawed. One started to stand. Neither one was the preacher.

"Don't get up," I said. I thumbed back the hammer on my Winchester and sort of pointed it at them. "Where's Preacher? Me and Doctor Puddin' Rawley is here to see maybe we take some women off your hands." I thought I heard one of the women suck in air. "Cash money, of course."

I believe both them men were near drunk.

One said, "He ain't here." He was slick-haired.

I smiled. "And I can see that. What I asked you was where he is."

The second man said, "I'm J-J-John. I'm i-i-in ch-ch-charge. P-P-Preacher . . ."

The first man said, "He's trying to say Preacher and Chico rode south to some Indian camp to see if they can sell off these three. Maybe get a medicine man to look at Chico. They oughta be back tomorrow."

Stuttering John stared pure murder at him. "I c-could've t-t-told th-that m-m-mys-s . . ."

I stepped back to the door. "Hey, Doc. Come on in. This is the place."

Slick said, "Yeah, yeah, you talk great. I'm glad to have somebody visit who can get out a sentence in less than twenty minutes."

Stuttering John went for his pistol and I shot him. He went sideways over his bench.

Slick yelled, "Hey! You shouldn't of ought to do that. He's . . ."

He was reaching for his pistol as he talked, so I shot him too. He went backward over the barrel he'd been sitting on.

Byden ran in about then and his wife saw him and she came running out hollering his name. I was kind of wired tight right then so I can't say whether she called him Pudding or Rawley. What I can remember clear is that she sort of hopped over Stuttering John to get to Byden, and that was unfortunate as it blocked my view of the bandito for an instant.

I saw his Colt coming up and pushed her aside as he fired. I put out my left hand to stop it, and of course that didn't work so good. Hell, it didn't work at all. And then he fired again.

CHAPTER NINE

I got my carbine untangled from the woman's skirts and got off another shot one-handed about the same time as the stutterer. Mine kind of skidded off his bench and took him in the leg.

I didn't think my left hand could hurt any worse, but be dadblamed if his second shot didn't hit that same hand, and it hanging limp beside me. I mean, it wasn't even in the fight. I yelled something awful and dropped the carbine as I couldn't work the lever and went for my Colt.

I got it out and cocked, but not before he was ready for his third shot. Right then, though, Byden got the woman clear and nailed Stuttering John to the floor with one of them big Spencer slugs. It took care of him. He didn't twitch much, and lucky for me his third shot went wild. It zinged off one wall and thunked into another, adding adobe chunks and dust to the fracas.

All this went down in a couple of seconds I guess, but it sure seemed like forever. Couldn't see squat for the gunsmoke, and everybody was yelling because we was all deaf from all the gunfire in that little hut.

I mean, all except the young Mex girl, because she was already deaf. She must of been able to feel the gunfire though, as she had slipped under one of them beds and was holding her ears. And crying.

I had a couple of thoughts right then, right clear.

First off, Byden's wife was a lot younger than him, and was the prettiest woman I'd ever laid eyes on. Even with dirty clothes

47

and tears cutting paths through the grime on her face, she was enough to stop a train. Her hair was light brown and she had the durndest blue-gray eyes you ever seen.

My second thought was that my left hand was ruint. Absolutely, totally ruint. Stuttering John's first shot had hit me in the palm and gone on through. His second slug had took off my knuckles and three fingers and left the little finger dangling and useless. I sort of gagged, just looking at it. I was in some kind of a fix.

I had a third thought then, although it wasn't so clear. I thought I was bleeding pretty bad, but then I passed out.

When I came back to my senses I was on one of them beds and the Mex girl was dabbing my face with a damp rag. She was a pretty thing, all cleaned up, and I thought if I was just ten years younger . . . and then I saw Byden's wife, cleaned up too, and that pretty little sweet deaf girl was gone from my mind. Emmalee, I remembered. I tried to say it.

Next thing I knew Byden's face was between us. He was bent over me, frowning like a momma bear. Blood all over his shirt.

"I don't expect you can talk much. You got to be dead hoarse from all that screaming, but that's all right. I don't appreciate your language in front of my wife. And I don't like how you was looking at her. Just 'cause she's been used hard don't mean you can treat her like a slut."

I can tell you that ain't no way to wake up. My hand had quit hurting so much, but it itched like crazy and when I went to scratch it, it was gone. What I had was a big old bandage with my thumb sticking out. No hand, no fingers. Gone.

Sunlight was pouring through the windows and I was soaking wet, yet I could see ashes smoldering in one of them Mex corner fireplaces. I tried to say I was hot, but it sounded more like I was coughing.

"Yeah, you're hot. Maybe fever, but probably from the fire. How you think I heated the water or sterilized my saw?"

I managed to get out a raspy, "Saw?"

Emmalee gave me a drink of cool water. Must of been a canvas water bag out back.

Byden frowned at her and said, "Yeah. I keep a folding saw in my possibles bag. Good thing I had it too. If you think that was fun with a saw, think on what it would of been like if I'd had to use your knife, cutting through bone and all."

The thought of that caused my balls to kind of draw up inside me.

I got another sip of water and wheezed. "Slick?"

"The slick-haired one? He died. Not before he told us the stutterer is Preacher's baby brother, though. Said if we thought Preacher was crazy mean before, just wait 'til he sees what we done here. Said he'll come after us and won't quit."

"Well, dang, Byden. I don't know as I can take any more good news."

CHAPTER TEN

We were making our way back into Santa Fe with the three women. We had a pair of bodies lashed on two of the extra horses, and were making pretty good time on the wagon road through the rocks and mesquite. Byden had got my arm in a sling, and I got myself on the outside of that half a jug of mescal that somehow survived all of the gun play. My missing hand had quit itching and gone to hurting like forty kinds of hell.

"Wish they'd of left more," I said as I tossed the empty jug on the roadside.

Byden said, "More of your hand or more of the liquor?"

"Liquor," I said.

"They did leave more," Byden said. "I poured a good bit on my saw and on what's left of your wrist and hand. Might head off infection. Might not. Anyways, I don't see why we didn't leave these bodies. We need to pick up Señora Terrazas and the boy and get away from here before that preacher gets after us."

"Might be paper on these two. We'll check with the town marshal." I was starting to slur. A little.

"Paper? What kind?"

"Ree-ward, that's what kind. Besides, ol' Preacher ain't gonna be near as hot to come after us, seeing as we picked up his buffalo guns from these dead yahoos."

We had captured a .50-90 Sharps Heavy and a .50-70 Long Tom along with some cash in the bandits' hacienda. About then I bumped my left wrist on my saddle horn and near screamed, but bit it back.

Emmalee saw me flinch and said, "Rawley, we need to stop and tighten up his sling."

I could have kissed her right then and there.

"What we need to do is to keep moving. Quit worrying so much about our poor baby here, and maybe he'll quit whining."

I could have killed him right then and there. I suppose the mescal had something to do with it, but anyways I stayed calm. My mare let go a pretty stout fart right about then, which helped too. Seemed like she was on my side.

"Ain't likely no rush anyhow," I said. "Preacher wasn't due back for another day or two. He comes back, finds them gone, he don't know who stole his money and women. Could have been other banditos. He comes into Santa Fe and asks the law, he runs into paper on himself and ol' Chico."

Byden snorted. "And how do you know there's 'paper' on them?"

"I'm getting ready to file it."

The marshal's office in Santa Fe was one more adobe building in a near solid adobe town. It didn't take long there. There was no paper on any of the preacher's gang, so I filed warrants on the two survivors and gave the marshal the sketch Billy had made. Not bad for a man who was cross-eyed drunk by that time.

The lawman pointed us to a doctor's office, and the medico took off the bandage Byden had done for me and put some more stuff on the stub. Burned like hot iron, but I managed not to yell. Could be I cussed some, but no more than you'd expect from someone in my miserable drunken condition. Missing a hand, and not yet twenty-four years old.

"Nice work there," the doctor said. "Especially that skin flap. I suppose it's good you saved the thumb. Useless as teats on a man now, but maybe if you can come up with some kind of false hand or hook or something . . ."

Something? I thought, *A daggone bear paw maybe?* He probably wasn't any more sober than me.

The doc started to rewrap the mess that once was my all-time favorite left hand, but Billy stopped him for a short look. He sort of measured my wrist with his fingers, then mumbled, "Sorry, Daddy."

The doc finished the bandage and said, "You seem sort of young to have a boy that old."

I hiccuped and said, "I certainly am. But it's good to have him around, as I'm a little short-handed right now."

I had me a good laugh over that one, but it didn't seem to perk nobody else up. Not even a little. I started to tell them that Billy was right handy, but good sense overtook me and I let that one go.

The four women went to use the marshal's privy one last time while Billy and Byden hitched up the wagon.

There was no question in my mind but I would be better off on my horse than bumping along in that wagon. None at all, until Miz Emmalee Byden climbed in and held out a hand to me.

I groaned pitifully and allowed her and Señora Terrazas to pull me in. Byden snorted again and stared a durn hole right through me.

Billy signaled to the deaf girl to see if she wanted to ride the wagon or a horse. When she shrugged, he pointed to a pony he'd saddled for her. She smiled, pushed her skirt between her legs, and swung neatly into the saddle.

Talk about a smile though, you had to see Billy right then. I might of looked right happy too, tucked in beside Miz Emmalee Byden.

★　★　★　★　★

We rode the rest of that day and much of the night. Some of it is still hazy to me as I got right feverish along the way. I do remember Emmalee swabbing me with my kerchief soaked in cold water. Leastways it seemed cold.

At some point I said, "How long did it take that second bandito to die?"

"He didn't simply die," Emmalee said.

"Do what?" I said.

"He didn't understand y'all had come to save us. He kept saying if y'all would save him, him and his friends would share. Said he'd explain to Preacher how y'all couldn't help killing his brother, as it was his brother's fault." She choked up a little, but went on. "Rawley was busy with you. When he . . . when that man started to describe how . . . what they had done to us . . . I couldn't . . ."

I could see why Byden had finished him off, and I didn't blame him.

Byden said, "You don't owe this boy no explanation, nor anyone else, neither. I don't want to hear no more talk about it. You hear me?"

Her eyes flashed but she went silent. It was much later when all the others was asleep in the wagon and I was half delirious, I heard her whisper to her husband. "Rawley Byden, you act as if I'm to blame. Like you're ashamed of me. I know you didn't let them take me, but I had no say-so either. Well, I'll tell you this. I am going to learn to shoot."

"Of course I didn't let anybody do anything. Are you crazy, woman? You think you're the only one hurt here in this mess?" He turned and looked back at her, his nose flared out and rage on his face. "And you don't need to worry about any more shooting. I will take care of you."

Talk about flaring. She went right back at him. What had

started as whispers got right loud. "Yes. And that's worked so well, hasn't it? You listen to me, Rawley, I could have maybe killed them several times. I even grabbed a pistol once and pointed it and squeezed the trigger. I didn't know you had to cock it first. They snatched it away and laughed at me. I will learn to shoot. And I will have my own pistol."

He hunched down and stared ahead.

I thought, *Me. Me. I'll teach you.*

Chapter Eleven

It was full dark when I woke up and realized we were parked in front of that Jesuit mission in Las Vegas. Wasn't hard to figure out since the entrance was well lit with a couple of oil lanterns. There was another lamp beside me in the wagon, along with the head Jesuit preacher. Old Hawk-Face himself, but his eyes was softer than I remembered.

"You probably shouldn't have moved him so soon," he said. "He has the fever. He may have the infection."

"Didn't have much choice," Byden said. "Some bad men is after us, and we got to keep as much distance as we can. We need to pick up the marshal and start home in the morning."

The Jesuit shook his head. "No. Neither of them is ready. You can all stay inside our walls and we will hide your wagon, or you can take the women and the boy and leave, but I insist these two men stay a little time longer."

I heard Curly Jack say, "How long?" and there he was, staring at me from the foot of the wagon.

The Jesuit shrugged.

I said, "Curly. Good to see you. How you coming along?"

"Better'n you, for dang sure. I ain't likely to lose any parts, anyways. How 'bout it, Padre? How long?"

The Jesuit said, "For you, you are weak, but soon. Tomorrow, the next day maybe. This young one? Not so soon. If the gangrene starts we must quickly take the rest of the arm."

"So, you figure him for gangrene, do you?" That was Byden.

I don't think he was hopeful. I ain't sure.

"I am hoping not. I smell nothing here," the Jesuit sniffed my wrist, "but we must watch and test with our noses for a few days. Can you not feel safe here?"

Byden said, "I don't know as I can ever feel safe again until I learn this Preacher Vance is stone dead and in the ground. Marshal, once you're up and rolling again, ain't you gonna take after the preacher? Pay him back for what he done to your woman?"

"I ain't through with him," Curly Jack said, but then he kind of lurched sideways and grabbed ahold of the wagon box with his good hand. It worried me no end, seeing him unsteady like that. I mean, Curly was kind of my personal Rock of Ages.

"You see?" the Jesuit fussed at him. "It has been only what, four days since you were shot? Your body must rest, gain strength. Billy, walk with him to his bed." To me he said, "Can you walk?"

"I surely can. Watch me."

I hopped out of that wagon bed, showing off a little for Miz Emmalee, took one step toward the mission, and passed out cold.

When I woke up on a straw mattress on the floor in Curly's room, my left arm was killing me. Must of landed on it. Being stupid ain't something so easy to fix. And my head hurt worse than my arm.

Come dawn, I struggled out to the privy, walking careful and holding on to things. Time I finished and headed back looking for food, there was Byden with the wagon, loaded and ready to roll.

Emmalee, Señora Terrazas, and her deaf daughter were aboard, along with the other Mex woman. The daughter, name of Conchita, was sitting by Byden. She was looking down at

Billy and patting the seat beside her. She had sort of a worried look, but it was still as comforting as that fresh sunrise, off hundreds of miles to the East.

Billy said, "No. Not now." He shook his head and pointed at me, then held up his left fist and pointed to it. The girl nodded like she understood, and he said, "Daddy, too," and pointed back to the mission.

I'm sure he meant Curly Jack, and no sooner did he say it when the marshal come out, walking slow himself, nursing a mug of coffee. A soft breeze nudged the steam away from his face and spread the smell over all of us.

"Marshal," Byden said. I noted that he hadn't spoke to me, but his wife did lay a nice smile on me. From behind him, sort of. Worried, maybe. My Lord, she was pretty.

"I see you won't wait," Curly Jack said. "I can't make you. All right then. Go straight at the morning sun, keep the afternoon sun dead behind you. Right on across the South Canadian 'til you come up on that trash-mouth widow's place, then—"

Byden cut hm off. "Yeah, Marshal, I know. Cross back to the south side of the river there, and follow it back to Tascosa. I got it."

The marshal shrugged and said, "Well, good."

Byden said, "I set them two buffalo guns and cartridge belts inside there, as well as all them spare pistols. I hope y'all don't mind me taking a couple of the horses along as spares."

I said, "Long as you left us our three and a packhorse, we'll be fine. Ought to let me go get one of them pistols for your wife, though." I wasn't trying to tick him off, honest, but that wasn't how he took it.

"She don't need no damn pistol," Byden near shouted, "and y'all can hurry up and get off your asses and go kill those bastards." He popped those reins hard, and they pulled away.

Marshal Curly Jack Sentell smiled at me and said, "Well, sir, listen to him. Talk about a trash-mouth."

That day they left is still much of a blur to me. The fever would come and go, as would the pain, but what thoughts I had was on Emmalee Byden, mainly.

I know, I know, she was married, and she had not made one single move toward me. Still, she seemed to care. And she was sure enough married to that old jerk-wad who didn't seem to know what a prize he had.

One minute I was wanting him gone, next I was eat slam up with guilt because he saved my arm. Or maybe my life.

Then again, I wished somebody had saved my durn hand. You ever tried to handle the buttons on your trousers one-handed? My life was changing faster than I ever wanted, and I wasn't all that old.

The next morning as we were washing up our bowls from breakfast, Curly Jack said, "Brodie, I think I've had about all the breakfast mush I can handle."

I said, "What do you want to do, Marshal? I don't want to hurt no Jesuit's feelings, but I don't see how we ever get our strength back eating nothing but soup and tomato sauce on them dumplings, child's food such as that."

"Strap on your pistol," he said. "We're going into town and find us some eggs and bacon. Ham, maybe. Biscuits and butter."

I must of grinned a mile wide. "If you're waiting on me, you're backing up. Maybe, time we finish, it's noon and time for some burnt steak and beans. Canned tomatoes and beer."

He said, "Now you're talking, Deputy. And afore we come back here to rest up, we see can we get ourselves some *chili con carne*. Personal, I like mine kind of hot. Spicy hot."

"How hot?" I knew he wanted me to ask.

"My butt oughta let me know it's time for supper when it quits burning from breakfast."

I felt good until I tried to strap on my pistol. Finally, I tucked it in my trouser waist. So did the marshal, I noticed.

"How you figure we gonna eat all this fine food, do we find it?" Now, I asked this in all earnestness. "Maybe Billy helps us? I mean, it ain't like sipping soup with a spoon."

Sentell studied me a moment. "Sorry, Brodie. I didn't mean to point up your problem. Leastways, I do have some use of my left hand. It ain't plumb gone like your'n. I think you got the right idea. We take Billy, and he can cut stuff up for us, butter the bread."

I said, "That's fine, if we find him. I ain't hardly seen hide nor hair of him lately."

The marshal said, "He's been busy. Got something he's been working on with some gunsmith. Wanted to show you hisself, but me telling you won't change nothing."

Curly Jack pulled a slip of paper from a pocket and passed it to me. It was a drawing. Looked like a tin can with rope strands and open on the one end, and two horns sticking out the other end.

"What in God's earth is this?" I said.

"Might be your new hand," Curly said. "Billy's been working on this. Let's see if he's here or off putting this together."

Billy walked in about that time. The marshal said, "Go ahead, Billy, show him the durn thing. The claw, I mean. Is it about ready?"

Billy reached under Sentell's cot and brought out this tomato can. There was a two-pronged hook, some garden tool I guess, sticking out the top. Billy proceeded to slip it on my stub. There was a padded slot cut out for my thumb, and there was padding inside too, so's it wouldn't ride too hard on what was left of my hand. Some leather thongs was tied into holes in the open end so's it could be lashed to my arm above the elbow. It looked like the sketches.

"Where in the hell did you find this?"

"Billy made it," Curly Jack said. "Does it work, having them prongs opposite your thumb?"

"It does." I was amazed. "I mean, I can pick some stuff up. Hold reins and such."

"Put out your own eye, do you go to scratch it." Curly laughed like the devil at his own joke. Billy got it too, after I made like I poked myself in the eye.

"A little loose on my forearm, and my wrist ain't ready for it yet. Still too sore, but my God, Billy . . ."

"Here," he said. "Off. Give me."

I slipped it off and handed it over. Billy stuffed some more cloth scraps in the top end as cushioning, then pointed at Curly Jack's leather wrist cuff.

The marshal said, "Good idea, Billy, durn good idea." He peeled off his left hand cuff and slipped it on my damaged arm, then helped Billy put the claw on again. With the cuff it was as good as it could get. Fit better, and the open end wouldn't cut up my shirt.

"Step back," I said. "Watch this." I drew my Colt and laid it between those two prongs to steady it. "You see? I think my carbine might fit this too. Billy, pass me my Yellowboy."

The prongs were too close together for the carbine's forestock to drop between them. Billy snatched my new claw off, took my carbine, and was out the door before I could say squat.

"He's heading for the gunsmith shop," Curly Jack said. "C'mon. Place I got in mind to eat at is right past there. We'll pick him up on the way and feed him too."

The gunsmith said he'd heat up those prongs and spread them to handle my carbine, and we could pick the claw up in a couple of hours.

There was a mercantile next door so we went in and got me my own wrist cuff, so's I could turn the marshal's back to him.

From there it was a stone's throw to Rosa's Cantina, where we loaded up on fried eggs and ham, with tortillas, peppers, beans, and what I think was probably ground-up prairie dog meat. Like I said, my Mex ain't all that good.

My claw wasn't quite ready, so the gunsmith sent us to a hotel that served pies and coffee. I had peach and Billy and the marshal had apple.

Feeling ten pounds heavier, we picked up my claw and carbine and plodded back to the mission for a two-hour siesta.

When Billy woke me up saying, "Daddy. Daddy, wake up," I thought I was dreaming about how this whole trip started.

I wasn't dreaming.

"Preacher," Billy said, his forehead scrunched up in worry. He pointed to the door. "Here."

CHAPTER TWELVE

Curly Jack heard him too, and we were both upright with pistols drawn in seconds.

The marshal whispered, "Where? In the mission?"

Billy shook his head, "Front. Not in."

"Don't seem like your warrants took, do it, Deputy?"

"It don't," I said. "I hate that. Can't let him see Billy, if he ain't already."

Curly said, "Did he see you when you seen him, Billy?"

Billy shook his head and said, "No."

"Certain sure?"

Billy nodded. It was plain he was scared, but heckfire, he'd seen this man cut his momma's throat. He was holding that little pistol I'd given him.

Curly Jack said, "I'm gonna take off my badge and go see what he's up to. He don't know me, and I ain't been in Santa Fe in five years. He knows Billy and maybe he's heard about a one-handed man, so y'all hunker down here."

He stuck a Schofield in his belt in front and the second one in the small of his back. He said, "Back in a few minutes," and started out but stopped in the door. "Best you don't let nobody in but me. You hear shooting, come on out and lend a hand," and he was gone.

It was right tense for fifteen minutes or so. I don't believe you could have drove a one-penny nail up my butt with a eight-pound hammer, not knowing how Preacher had ducked arrest and found us, or how many men he had.

Still, I had to act calm for Billy's sake, so I did.

Finally, there came a tap-tap on the door. Me and Billy stood clear in case they shot through it, but then we heard the marshal say, "It's me and the padre. Don't shoot."

I undid the bolt but kept the doorway covered until we saw clear that they were alone.

"He still outside?"

Curly Jack said, "Naw. You can stand down some. Decock them pistols. He's gone, leastways for now. The padre here didn't want to lie, I guess, so he played dumb. '*No comprende,* Señor.' I lied like a dog. Told him you had been in Las Vegas, since he was looking for a one-handed lawman and you surely been seen. I told him you'd done gave up your badge and gone north to look for a cushy job with the railroad."

"He alone?"

Curly Jack gave me a funny look. "He'd been alone, I'da killed him. Naw, Brodie, he had three men with him. One was a Mex with a limp, must have been that Chico. Big man. Had another scrawny Mex with bone-handled Colts, and the last one was a bushy-whiskered old fart with a long Remington. Out of work buffalo runner was my take."

I was feeling some better, but not much.

"How we gonna even those odds?" I asked.

"We'll worry on that later. I asked 'em if they was looking for another shooter, to kinda throw 'em off. The preacher said he didn't really need nobody else, but if I's interested in a share of whatever they could put together, I could catch 'em up in the railroad camps. If I came on pretty quick."

I said, "How come he didn't tell you to saddle up right now?"

Curly Jack smiled. "He did, sort of. I said I was getting over a gunshot wound and these Eye-talian doctors needed to take out my stitches before I could ride. Needed another day or two, maybe."

"Fast thinking, Marshal."

"Yes, it was, Deputy. And now I think we get ourselves ready to head back to Texas, soon as they's gone. Hook up with Byden and them women again."

"How come?"

The marshal frowned. "Because he also said that soon as he found you and killed you he was going to Texas to find a wagon full of women and take 'em back again. Maybe by the time he catches up to us we'll be fit to deal with him."

I said, "Odds will be better too. With Byden, it's four against three."

Billy said, "Against four. Me."

CHAPTER THIRTEEN

The sun was a couple of hours past noon and a dry wind was blowing. The marshal disappeared for a while as me and Billy were getting set to go. Billy helped me lash down my slicker and bedroll, and I tucked my carbine in its scabbard.

I said, "It's hot enough to bake bread in my throat, Billy."

He said, "Drink some."

I did. He gave me a right harsh frown, then bent to check my cinch.

"Meant water," he mumbled.

When the marshal came back he took his pommel holster with those two Schofields and slapped the whole rig on my horse.

"These are a sight easier to load and reload than a Colt or Remington," he said. "Half-cock it, push the release latch against your leg like so, it pops right open. Push the top of the barrel on your leg and it ejects your empties. Stick the barrel up under your other arm and you can reload it, all one-handed, then push the bottom of the barrel against your leg, saddle, whatever, and it locks into place. That Schofield feller made the latch change on the big Smith and Wessons so's a horseman could do all this while handling his reins with his off hand."

"Lucky for me," I said, even though I wasn't feeling lucky at all. "Excepting the fact that my off hand is off. I guess if I had to reload on the run I could hold my reins in my teeth."

He said, "I wouldn't try it on horseback 'less I was truly

hard-pressed. Good way to lose a pistol."

"What about you?"

"I'll wear a pair of them Colts you took off them banditos you killed. Stick some of these Schofield cartridges in your pistol belt and put the rest in your saddle pockets. And I got two more boxes, case you want to practice some once we're away from here."

I said, "Why? Why're you hanging onto Schofield cartridges, if you're giving me the pistols?"

"I didn't say nothing about giving 'em to you. Think on 'em as a loan. Main thing is that I can run Schofield cartridges through these Colts, though the vicey versus ain't true."

The padre showed up then with a bag of corn dodgers, some jerky, two loaves of bread, some tinned ham, and a sack of coffee beans. Curly Jack gave him five dollars for it and for taking us in.

"That is not needed," the padre said, but he tucked away that sawbuck pretty durn quick. "The bad men have ridden north, but you should know that a rider has come from Santa Fe to report that two lawmen were killed there two days ago."

I said, "So?"

"By someone dressed as a minister."

"Oh."

The marshal said, "Your warrants probably got them two killed, Brodie."

I said, "You would of done it different?"

"Nope. I wasn't talking you down, Deputy. You done right. I'da done the same, so I guess you could say them two deaths is on both of us. It's some more payback the preacher is due."

I said, "What if he don't come after us?"

"He will. Y'all killed his sad-assed stuttering brother. But say he don't. Soon as I'm up to the mark again, I'm going after him."

"Well, I'll be with you. Count on it."

Billy said, "Me too."

We rode east with maybe four hours of daylight left. Billy was trailing two packhorses behind him, as neither me nor the marshal were up to pulling a spare as yet. Those two were mainly spares anyways since we didn't have too much to pack. Those two buffalo guns, of course, extra ammunition and canteens, some vittles and cook pots and a durn shovel, but mainly Curly Jack wanted to make sure we didn't wind up riding double again.

"A durn shovel?" I said. "I hope you ain't counting on me to be digging no ditches."

He didn't laugh. "Might have to bury someone, and I ain't counting on you for much, but don't go getting sorry for yourself on me. You been dealt a bad hand but you got to play the hand you're dealt."

"I'd just as soon you quit talking about hands, Marshal."

My arm still wasn't ready for my claw, so the arm was back in a sling and the claw was wrapped up in a spare shirt in one saddle pocket. Billy had tied my reins together, one more thing necessary but needing some getting used to. Leastways now I could hook them on my left thumb or over my saddle horn, so's to free up my right hand. To grab some jerky or a pistol. Bottle, maybe. Rub my eyes. Scratch.

Fever was gone but the pain wasn't, and sometimes the headaches near made me crazy. I knew I didn't have any business on a long trail ride, but what choice did I have? Anyways I did have two bottles of rye wrapped up in my other saddle pocket. And part of a bottle in my belly. The marshal had bought them.

"Where'd you come up with all this wealth you're spreading around, Marshal? Sweetwater mailed you some salary?" Liquor will make me false cheerful at times.

"Sold off the tack from them two dead banditos and one horse."

"Wasn't there also some cash from them renting out the women?"

"There was, for a fact. I got it from Byden and gave it to the women. Byden didn't want to let me have it at first but we came to an agreement when I pushed a Colt up against his stones."

I snorted, "He's probably already took it back. Emmalee's share, at least."

"Maybe," he said. "But we was alone when this went down and I told him if he did and I learned of it, we'd have another little talk."

"You're a good man, Marshal. I don't care what others might say."

"You been drinking, so you go on with your smart mouth, but try and register what I'm fixing to tell you, Brodie. I seen how you was looking at Miz Byden and so did him and anybody else."

"So? A man can't look? You don't think she's something to look at?"

Curly Jack turned in the saddle to lock eyes with me. "You know what I'm saying. What you was doing was more than taking a sideways admiring peek at a good-looking woman. Which I grant you, she is. But you get between her and Byden, and he kills you, he's justified in my eyes. And I'm the law."

The rye whiskey stiffened my back and bowed me up a little. "That so, Marshal? And what if he don't kill me? What if I kill his sorry bossy ass?"

"Well, Deputy, I guess that would mean that I don't know you no better than Billy's house cat. I'd arrest you for murder and fatal stupidity."

"You serious, Curly?"

"I purely am."

I could see he was. It made me right mopey, so I said, "Well, it don't matter none, since she ain't shown one single ounce of interest in me."

"See, Brodie, I don't know as that's so. I seen her look at you too. You're young, more like her than him. You ain't total ugly and you saved her. And you got the pity angle. But don't none of that matter, unless she cuts him loose. You mark me?"

"Yes, I mark you, dammit."

"Hell, Brodie, she's as close to a lady as you're gonna see out here. Pity is probably all you got going for you, now that I think on it."

"You made your point, Marshal. I don't want to talk about it no more." I felt lower than catfish droppings and the more I thought on it, the further down I drooped. I couldn't find any holes in what the marshal had said.

That was then. As you might expect, things got worse.

CHAPTER FOURTEEN

We made good time the rest of that day and half the next. I burned a dozen rounds through the Schofields along the way, to see how they sighted. And to practice the reloads, of course, which wont easy at all. Dumping the empties was no problem, but I had to hold the open gun against my chest with my nub to drop in fresh rounds. That would get a sight easier once I could wear my claw.

The Schofields were all right, but nothing fits my hand like a Colt. I still had mine, but there was no way I could reload it. Heck, I couldn't even put on my pistol belt by myself. I pulled most of the forty-four Henry rounds from my belt and dropped them in my saddle pocket. Replaced them with Schofield forty-fives.

On the last ridge before we dropped down to the South Canadian, Billy pointed behind us and said, "Look."

Might have been the whiskey, but I couldn't see jack-squat without my scope, and my horse was dancing some. I mean, I saw some dots on the plains behind us, but they was about as big as tick turds.

The marshal had his scope on them long before I could fumble mine out one-handed.

"I make six riders and eight horses. Take a look through this, Billy." He tossed the glass to the boy as I got mine steady on my left arm.

"Durn, Billy, how'd you spot them with your plain eyes?"

He shrugged at me. I've heard deaf people can smell better than most and blind folks can hear better. Maybe since Billy was kicked silly, his sight was extra good to make up for it. Who knows?

Billy said, "Preacher."

Curly Jack said, "Shit. And durn if he ain't got some more help."

I said, "How'd they get onto us so fast?"

"Don't know and it don't matter," Curly Jack said. "We're gonna change directions, head south this side of the river, over toward Tucumcari Mountain. Try to make 'em think we're bound for Wichita Falls, maybe."

"Then what?"

"We turn north past the mountain, cross the Canadian and go back to Tascosa that way. Try to lose 'em when we duck behind the hill. They's some slab rock thereabouts, which is precious hard to track over."

"And if we don't lose 'em?" I couldn't make heads nor tails of his plan so far, but I had been drinking. A little.

"Well, Deputy, then we turn and fight 'em. Ambush 'em at the river. We got three good long guns. All's we got to do is kill a couple of 'em and that changes everything. Maybe knock down two or three horses."

"Why don't we do that now?" See, I wasn't being stubborn. Just drunk.

"Well, Deputy, since I'm your boss and we're gonna do it my way, let's ride while I try and settle your drink-frazzled mind."

We got underway.

He continued. "I want 'em to think we're heading for Wichita Falls, so's they don't figure out we're going toward Tascosa. They pick up on that and then it's a horse race on who gets to that wagon full of women first."

I said, "Oh. They could split up."

"Good to see your brain ain't been eaten totally by demon rum. Now, let's go hard."

We did, and kept going come dark, but slowed down a bunch. Last we saw of them we'd gained a mile or two.

"You think they'll ride through the night too, Marshal?" I was stone sober by then.

"Naw," he said. "Can't. They're tracking us. They'll have to break for the dark. I only hope we don't stumble on some prairie dog village and break a leg."

Come dawn we were plodding along, all dozing in the saddle, and the sunrise woke us up.

Curly Jack said, "That's Tucumcari Mountain off to the left some. We'll head for it but we want to pass to the right of it before we turn north. Let's take a break here, have some coffee and jerky and water the horses."

As I was swinging down I said, "What are those mountains behind it?"

Curly Jack was already down, pouring canteen water in his hat for his horse. He laughed and said, "Ain't no mountains behind it."

I said, "Well, Mister Know-It-All, take another look."

He did and said, "Shit." Second time in two days, and he was not a cussing man.

I said, "What now?"

He said, "That ain't no mountain range at all. I wish it was, but it's a dadgum sandstorm. We got to ride." He mounted and thundered off.

Me and Billy caught him in a couple hundred yards. Looked to me like he was riding right into that durn dust cloud. He must have read my mind.

"It's blowing south and west," he yelled. "We'll try to skirt it on the south side. Try to miss most of it, anyways. If we make it, it'll cover our tracks complete. Pull up your scarves and stay close."

We pounded along the edge of that moving wall of sand for maybe five miles and caught a good bit of dirt ourselves. All of a sudden though, we were moving in opposite directions. It was roaring off to our rear and we were riding into bright sunlight, with the storm off on our left, stretching away as far as we could see.

The marshal slowed to a walk. He dropped his scarf and said, "It looks to be following the Canadian. And it ought to plumb bury them banditos chasing us."

I said, "Marshal, that was a right smart move, for an old bald man. I don't know how you came up with that. Never seen anything like it."

He said, "If I ain't wrong, they's a creek in them trees a mile or two south. We'll water up there, rest the horses a bit."

The creek was there. "How'd you know that?" I asked. I was right impressed about then.

He smiled and said, "Magic."

"Naw, Marshal, come on. I'm trying to learn. How'd you know, by the line of trees?" See, water is mostly sparse in the Panhandle and that part of New Mexico Territory. There'd been awful droughts in the mid-seventies.

"Well, a good tracker would have noticed that line of trees, meandering toward the river. Like you said, that's a good sign of water. Matter of fact, that's how my Ranger pardner Tom Duffy found this creek, last time I was here."

The booger was grinning ear to ear. He'd been here before and hadn't even been the one to find the creek in the first place. He got me good.

"Why were you here? I know durn well you want me to ask."

"It's kind of you to ask, Deputy. Me and Tom were tracking a party of Kioway horse thieves, maybe ten years back. We crossed the Canadian and followed 'em to right here, this very spot. They had watered up here, and we were reading their sign. Tom says, 'Durn, Sergeant, they's at least six or seven of 'em. You think we oughter be chasing that many?' I says, 'Heck, Duffy, they's two of us, right?' While we were laughing, about a hundred of 'em came screaming across the prairie. All right, it was seven of 'em, same as we'd been tracking, but they had the bulge on us. We left our packhorse and rode like hell back to Tucumcari Mountain." He stopped to put on the coffee.

"What then?"

He gave me this look, serious as a case of the pox. "Heckfire, Deputy, they was seven of them and only two of us. What do you think happened? They wiped us out."

Billy was giggling and spitting. Me? There was smoke coming off my head, and the marshal could see I didn't like being made fun of.

"All right, all right . . . I had a Henry and Tom had a Colt rifle. Short rifle, five-shooter. We got up on that little mountain and smoked 'em pretty good. When he started plugging their horses with them big-ass fifty-six-caliber slugs, they decided to go elsewhere whilst they still had more horses than they started with."

"You keep on trailing them?"

"Deputy, are you bat-shit crazy? We called it a good patrol and went home. Reported that out of them seven raiders, we'd killed thirteen. Maybe fourteen."

Chapter Fifteen

"I bet I'm three pounds lighter."

We had watered up, ate a bite, and shook a good part of New Mexico Territory out of our clothes. There was so much sand around us when we finished it could have been a beach, back on the Gulf of Mexico. I said so.

Billy said, "Beach?"

"I heard of 'em, but never seen one," said Curly Jack. "It's the dirt edge of a ocean, Billy. Lily-white sand, so I heard."

"I went once," I said. "It ain't all lily white. Lots of sea-shells mixed in. And it's salty. The water is, I mean."

"Seashells?" Billy asked.

"Yeah, Billy," I said. "There's lots of critters in the ocean, other than fish. They got shells on 'em."

Curly Jack took off his hat and scratched his noggin. "Like a armadillo?"

"Sort of, Marshal, or a turtle maybe, only harder. They last almost forever, even after the critters die."

"My Lord. How big?" The marshal was asking, but both him and Billy looked like they were having trouble swallowing all this.

"Some as small as your thumbnail," I said. "Some bigger than your fist. Some hunker down inside the shells, like caves. Others got hinges they can open and close."

"Nunh-uh!" said Billy.

The marshal said, "So, they'd be like mussels. I seen them in creeks back east as a boy. Look, Brodie, I could listen to this all day and Billy likes it too, but we need to get moving. You can run off at the mouth while we ride."

"All right," I said. "Which way?"

"We'll go straight north. Can't be more'n a half-day to the South Canadian, and we'll be near to the spread of that vile widow and her noisy son."

I said, "We ain't going back into that mess, surely?"

"I think we need to check on 'em, Brodie. I purely do. They might of been buried too."

We headed north. "There is still enough wind whipping around to blow the loose sand over our tracks in no time, so even did them banditos not get buried, ain't no way they can track us. I don't see why we got to go back and listen to them two no more." I guess I wanted to hear myself talk, as Curly Jack Sentell was going to do whatever he set out to do, and wasn't no talk of mine going to sway him.

"I was serious about maybe digging them out," he said. "You must of not been through a bad storm like this. I have. Caught three of us Rangers on a chase once, up near to Beaver Creek on the way to Camp Supply. We made it to a shack, got inside, and sat it out."

"Horses?" Billy said.

"They was inside with us, Billy. It blew a day and a half, and wasn't hardly no place to lay down, what with all the horse droppings. Blew dirt through every durn crack in that shack. We had to keep our scarves up the whole time. When it finally let up, I jerked that door open and half the durn Indian Territory caved in on me. It was head-high outside the door. There was enough opening for the three of us to crawl up and push and pull and get one another out, but then we didn't have nothing to dig out the horses with, and they was snorting to get out."

I said, "What did you do, use your hands?"

"Tried that. Too slow, too much sand. I had to crawl back inside, cut them leather hinges on the door, and push it back outside. We broke it up, used the boards to shovel out the horses."

"Durn," I said. "No, I never seen such as that. What were you doing up in the Territory?"

"Chasing two half-breed horse thieves. I ain't ever worried too much about boundaries on a chase."

"You don't say." I mean, he's a Texas town marshal and he's telling me this in New Mexico Territory.

My humor went right over his head.

"Pure truth," he said. "Anyways, we come out better than the breeds we was chasing. Caught up to 'em two days later. They had sheltered in a cabin too, but left the four horses tied outside. Horses had broke loose and made it to the creek, then come back after the storm to wait on their masters. They would'a waited a long time, too, as that rickety cabin had caved in on them boys. We could tell by the smell."

"You dig them out?"

"No need. They was mostly buried. Good enough for bandits, anyways. We took their horses and tack back as proof we got 'em, but our captain said it wasn't good enough. Said the dead smell coulda been one bandit, or maybe a total stranger."

"What did you do?"

"I told him if he ever saw either one of 'em alive, let me know and I'd kill 'em again. That didn't set all that well with him, and that's how I come to be the law in Sweetwater. Now, I want to hear more about them shellfish."

Billy said, "Yes!"

"Well," I said, "The big ones was called conks. They dug one out of the bank of this little creek, right there in the dunes . . ."

"Dunes?"

"Sand hills on the beach. They took this conk and smashed

the shell, and here's this big, old white injia-rubber looking thing. They boiled it some to clean it, then diced it up and fried it with batter. Made conk fritters. Pretty durn good, too. And they made a kind of soup with it, too. Milk, 'taters, butter, onions . . ."

And so we passed the time on the ride to the South Canadian. We made it by dark, and camped on the north bank. We had a dinner of jerky and cold corn dodgers and was asleep in no time.

CHAPTER SIXTEEN

Once again, I woke up with Billy in my face, but this time he was grinning and saying, "Fish."

I could smell it before I could focus on it. It was a catfish and a nice one at that. Had to be six or seven pounds, and he was holding it about six inches from my face.

Billy took my knife and pinned that cat's head to a tree, then used his blade to slice around the head. He peeled off the skin and deboned that fish neat as you please, and pretty soon we had strips frying for breakfast. Refried a few dodgers to go with them.

Speaking of dodgers, that hard ride to dodge the storm about beat the snot out of both me and the marshal. Wont neither of us well men to start with. I'm certain sure that's the only reason we were being chased instead of the other way around.

If that Preacher Vance thought he was due some vengeance over his brother, he had no idea how bad Curly Jack hated him. Billy felt the same but couldn't say as much.

If them two hadn't been strapped with a one-handed deputy and concerned over a wagon full of women, they'd of probably been taking on that gang head on, right then.

Could be I was saving their lives.

"Brodie, can you wear your claw yet?"

We had just broke camp. Well, they had broke camp. I did what I could, which wasn't much.

"I don't know. I'll try it, but it still feels tender."

I fished it out, dropped it, and Billy picked it up and helped me put it on. Or tried to, leastways.

"Too puffy," I said. "Won't slide on."

Billy sniffed and said, "Smells."

The marshal said, "That ain't good. Billy, take his pistol and cartridge belt and strap 'em on. Get his carbine and scabbard too."

"Whoa," I said. "Hold on a durn minute."

"You got my Schofields, Brodie. You can't work the Winchester without no claw and you can't reload a Colt. Billy will need 'em do we get in a scrape."

He was unpacking that trapdoor rifle while he spoke, along with a canvas belt loaded with .50-70's. He tossed the belt to Billy.

"Strap that on his waist. I'm gonna rig this Long Tom on your horse, Deputy. You can lean it on your left arm and load and shoot it one-handed. How you want it set up?"

"Might as well put it on the left side," I said, "So's I can grab it when I dismount. Ain't no way I can draw that monster whilst I'm in the saddle."

"Butt forward?"

"I guess. I don't know. Dammit all, I miss my hand."

"Yeah. Me too. Mount up, Deputy. We got to catch Byden and have him look at your nub. We'll find that ranch then cross back over, see can we pick up their tracks."

Exactly what I needed. Another hard ride.

Turned out the ranch was less than five miles east of our camp. We almost missed it. Durn near rode right between it and the river.

Would have, too, except Señora Terrazas and the other Mex woman was drawing water from the river and yelled at us. About startled the pure mess out of us.

Didn't none of us have any idea what they was yelling, and all three of us drew and covered them in a flash.

The marshal said, "Ain't that the Señora? First one we captured back? That one on the right?"

Billy nodded and I said, "I believe you're right, Marshal."

About then there was more yelling from uphill on our left, and a whole passel of folks descended upon us. Byden, Emma-lee, Conchita, the foul-mouthed widow, and both her sons. You never heard such carrying on.

When at last they let up, Curly Jack said, "Where's the ranch?"

The talkative son said, "Right there, under that mound of sand. You ain't never seen such a storm. We had to dig out a side winder. Door was fixed to swing outward, see, so we couldn't . . ."

The marshal interrupted him. "The wagon and horses?"

Byden answered. "Wagon is that mound on the right. Horses is gone."

The boy started again, or maybe he never let up. "Yessir, Mister Marshal, you ain't ever seen the likes. That mound on the left is where the shed was. You caught us all around back of the house, trying to dig down to the tool shed with our hands and some fry pans. You know, trying to get to some shovels . . ."

"Byden, you need to look at Brodie's arm. Right now. Billy says it's getting ripe."

CHAPTER SEVENTEEN

The marshal swung down and pulled that shovel from one of our packhorses and tossed it to the noisy son. Leastways we weren't burying somebody with it.

"Holler out when you get down to them other tools and some of us will help you dig out. Right now we got to see to my deputy."

The boy handed the shovel to his brother and said, "I'll let my brother do it, see, 'cause I'd really like to watch this. What happened to his hand? I ain't never seen no half a hand before. Can I . . ."

The marshal took a fry pan from Emmalee and handed it to the boy.

"Go help your brother. Nobody can think half-right with you yapping your durn head off."

"Yessir. Yessir, we'll hurry, but can I watch if'n you're gonna cut on him some more?"

"Go on. Git!"

I'd got down by then, and Byden was unwrapping my wrist. I was able to lock eyes with Emmalee over his shoulder as he worked. He wasn't exactly gentle, but I managed not to flinch. Much.

He made a face as the bandage came off, and I could see it myself. It smelled worse than it looked. I mean, it didn't smell all that bad. Nothing like a dead animal, but it was enough to draw flies right away.

I tried to shake them off but Byden held my arm tight and said, "Quit moving."

Emmalee got tight-lipped and scrunched up her nose, then said, "Are you going to have to cut more? Is it too late?"

I can tell you that those is several words you don't want to hear when you're talking about rot on your very own arm—"cut more" and "too late," I mean—but it was in fact too late. She had done said them.

My mouth went dry and my tongue swoll up. I couldn't talk and couldn't barely think. I sort of shriveled up inside myself.

"If we wasn't alongside this little river, I've no doubt I'd have to take the arm, at least up to the elbow."

The marshal said, "What's the river got to do with it?"

Byden said, "You won't find no blowflies up on the plains. They need two things. Dead meat to feed on as maggots, and damp earth to bury into to hatch into flies. These flies is laying hundreds of eggs as we speak."

I yanked my arm away. "You trying to kill me, you rotten dirty . . . ?" I was swatting flies hard as I could, but I wanted to swat him.

"I'm trying to save you. Lemme hold your arm again, and be still. Those eggs will hatch tomorrow and you'll have hundreds of baby maggots eating the dead meat off your hand and wrist. They don't eat live flesh. Three days later they're full, they drop off and bury in the ground, and you're cured. Maybe."

"He's right, Mister Dent. I've seen it with hurt sheep," Emmalee said, though she still looked worried and was biting a knuckle.

Curly Jack said, "Me too. Had a pack mule mauled by a panther once, up on the Washita. Had a half-breed Cherokee guide. Told me to let the mule lay up a few days, and durn if them worms didn't eat that wound clean."

"So I'm to set still and let a bunch of maggots hatch and eat on what's left of my hand?"

Byden said, "Only if you want to keep it."

"You don't pour likker on it?" the marshal asked. "Wrap it or nothing? I mean, he ain't a durn mule."

"Liquor would kill the eggs. Once they hatch into maggots and start feeding we'll put some kind of light cover over it so's he don't shake 'em off." Byden smiled at me and there wasn't a ounce of sweetness in it. "Bite your tongue and be still, Dent. Let 'em do their work. Might itch some. Could be right bad."

You know how it is when somebody tells you not to scratch some place. It commences to itch like crazy, every time. This was worse. And immediate.

The marshal did look sympathetic. He said, "Ain't no reason we can't pour some likker in him. I guess we'll keep him drunk for three days."

I said, "Four. I heard what he said. It's four days. Billy, dig me out a bottle from my saddle pockets."

He pulled one out and handed it to me and said, "Here, Daddy."

"I ain't your daddy, Billy. You got to stop that. You don't have a daddy nor a momma, just like me. They're dead and gone and you got to get over it." I know I snapped at him and it wasn't called for. I guess it was what I was going through myself.

I took a big swallow and went at him again. "And another thing. Don't go looking at the marshal. He ain't your daddy, neither. Heckfire, he don't have no momma nor daddy his own self. He's a orphan like you and me. Only older."

Billy hung his head and said, "Yes."

You can guess how bad I felt then. I suppose since I couldn't whack Byden over the head I took it out on Billy.

The marshal said, "Now, there's a good idea, Deputy. Beat up on Billy. Feel better now?"

Not exactly. Didn't help at all. The look Emmalee was giving me, I couldn't tell if she pitied me or despised me. Durn.

Chapter Eighteen

Only good thing about the next several days was I was too sick to help dig out from that sandstorm. Nobody else got to avoid it, not even Emmalee or the marshal, nor the foul-mouth old woman, and she'd been shot not even a week before me. Turns out her name was Bonnett.

I finished my whiskey by the third day but the marshal bought a jug of bust-head from the Bonnetts to get me through.

The liquor helped, but it was still a bad four days. I lifted up that bandage to peek the second day and it about froze my heart to see them hundreds of white grubs milling about on my nub. I swear I could close my eyes and hear them munching on me, though Emmalee said it wasn't so. She sat with me some, to feed me and listen to me rant, as long as Byden wasn't hanging over us.

And Billy. You know how a kicked dog will suck up to you after you mistreat it, trying to figure out what it did wrong and make it up to you? Even when it hadn't done nothing wrong? That was Billy.

He helped to feed me too, and watched over me as I washed off in the river, always signaling me to keep my nub up and dry. Stood by with my carbine whilst I did my business in the bushes downstream. Like the liquor and my situation hadn't brought me low enough, Billy being so nice generally made me feel like buffalo chips.

The fourth day the maggots had more than doubled in size

and were crawling out from under that bandage and dropping off pretty fast. Byden rinsed the rest of them off and poured some liquor on it, which stung to beat hell, but he said it looked good.

The others had finished digging out the house and wagon by then, no thanks to me, but we were still short on horseflesh. All we had were the mounts we rode in on and the two spares.

"We'd be all right," Curly Jack said. "We could harness two to the wagon and me and you and Billy would have mounts, but that leaves the Bonnetts flat."

I said, "You gonna leave them one of ours?"

He said, "Might have to. First off I'm gonna ride along the river a bit. Them horses and mules that was here went somewheres. Durn sure didn't fly away. Byden, you ride with me. Billy, you and these Bonnett boys keep an eye out."

Old Miz Bonnett cackled, "Y'all look out for our gosh-damn cattle too. Twenny, maybe twenny-five head of them sons-abitches is gone too."

As they rode off I heard the marshal say, "We'll go downstream first. Ride this side, then cross over after a few miles. Come back the other side and head upstream, if we ain't found nothing."

With Byden gone, Emmalee was a changed woman. Slow at first, but those next hours were the start of hope for me.

Right off, though, she lit me up. "I can't believe how you've treated Billy since you got here. Like a red-headed stepchild, and him doting on you and the marshal like you were each his real daddy."

"Well," I started, "I . . ."

"I don't care that you were drunk. It's no excuse. My daddy was a drinking man, but he never was mean to us. If you can't handle whiskey without it changing you, you need to let it go."

"I have run dry, so . . ."

"That does not count, Brodie Dent. Don't be stupid. I never knew you before you were shot, but Marshal Curly says you are not stupid. At least, not when you're sober. I wouldn't know."

"What do you mean?"

"Exactly what I said. You've been shot up and drunk since five minutes after you strolled into my life. I can't but wonder what you were like before I met you."

That backed me up some. She kept going.

"I know what all you've done. The marshal talked while we were digging. Saved my husband, saved Señora Terrazas, saved the marshal, found us and saved us. Even my husband let some of it out, though he resents you something awful now."

"But why, Emmalee? What've I done to him?"

"He is not confident in himself. He won't say as much, but I think it's why he moved us from Michigan to a tiny Mexican goat-herder village in the middle of nowhere."

"Why'd you come? I mean, I'm glad you did, but it's a total surprise to find you out here, so smart and nice and pretty . . ."

I said more than I meant to, but she didn't seem to dislike it. Fact is, she blushed as red as a plum.

"Please do not forget I'm married, Mister Dent." She said that, but she smiled and her eyes said, "Thank you very much."

I stammered something, and she said, "I believe the liquor makes you bold. At any rate, I was married to him back then too. My father was killed at Gettysburg and I had five sisters. My mother was pleased to marry me off and lose one mouth, even though Mister Byden was my father's friend. He is much older than us, Brodie."

Us. She said *us.* I said, "He can't be worried about me. A one-handed lawman with no prospects?"

She gave me a funny look. "If you are going to continue wallowing in your pity like a hog in slops, no one will need worry about you. You will lead a dismal life and die alone."

And she stood and walked away. Left me sitting there on the ass-end of that wagon, alone like she said, and feeling like I'd gut-shot myself.

Ouch.

She wasn't gone more than fifteen minutes, but that was long enough for me to slide into a deep depression.

I had never been hooked on one woman before. There'd been a half-dozen or so, all working girls, that I'd enjoyed being with. I might of settled with any one of them, was I older and less footloose and had an actual stash.

This wasn't the same. I was really down and it wasn't even entirely because I'd run out of whiskey. I felt like I'd run out of chances too, at least as far as Emmalee Byden was concerned. I hopped down and turned to go to the soddy and there she was, walking back out to the wagon.

"Go back and sit yourself down, Mister Dent. I only went to get you a bite to eat."

My second life began right then, though I didn't know it at the time. It was not nearly as easy as my first life, but it was much better. Leastways after a while.

CHAPTER NINETEEN

She fed me. It wasn't nothing but jerky and a can of stewed tomatoes, but I think it was the best meal of my life up to that point. She made me try to use my thumb and claw to hold the spoon and I maybe got one spoonful out of three to my mouth, but it did cause us both to laugh.

She talked a lot and it seemed like every time I got set to say something stupid she'd shove some food in my mouth, so the whole thing worked right well. She talked, I listened.

"You've been hurt badly, but you did it saving me. I mean, us. Me and the Mexican women. You have to learn to take pride in that, like a war wound. Wear it like a medal, and use it. Make Billy proud of your new hand, Brodie. It is amazing, what he did, and he seems to worship you like an older brother."

I started to say how much I missed my own brother, but she shoved another piece of jerky in my mouth.

"And Marshal Sentell, he acts like you might be his son, as well as Billy. Don't you see how it pains him to see you so low and so hard on Billy?"

I nodded and tried to swallow, but that strip of dried beef wasn't nowheres near ready to go down.

"You won't grow another hand, Brodie, and you won't get better until you learn to refuse pity. You must become the best one-handed lawman of the region and earn everyone's respect for it. Do you really want people to feel sorry for you? Me, for example?"

I realized right then that it would kill me, and I started on the come-back trail.

I took a deep breath and said, "So, if I become the best damn lawman around, one-handed or not, maybe I'd have a chance at your good graces?"

"Perhaps if you watch your language. I know you can do better," she said. "I've seen you in action. And Marshal Sentell needs you to be that man. We all do. We don't know when the preacher is coming."

I nodded, and felt a chill. "But we do know he's coming."

"I'll help all I can," she said. "You know I must respect my husband's feelings too, so what I can do may be limited."

"I don't mean to cause you problems with him," I said. I'm not sure I meant it.

"You are the problem, Brodie, but it's not your fault. He sees you as a danger. He fears I will run off with you."

"You know that?"

"He has said so. I told him that he is the only person that can run me off. He's a hard man, but he's done his best for me, and I take my vows seriously."

I nodded again. Not what I wanted to hear, but what I had come to expect from her. I had already heard much the same from the marshal, but it didn't hit so hard as coming from her.

"Billy!" I yelled at the house. "Bring me that little pistol I gave you."

He did, and I topped off that five-shooter and gave it to her. I said, "I'm gonna teach you to shoot."

I did, too. Took a broke-off six-by-one board from the remains of the horse shed and set it up down by the river. Taught her about sighting and showed her to hold it two-handed, cocking with her left thumb. Billy stayed to watch. Didn't really bother me none as I wasn't getting anywhere with her noways.

"Try and put your sights on his belly," I said. "Middle of the board. That way if your shot goes high it hits him in the chest and if you pull it down some you hurt him even worse."

She didn't blush. She got a serious frown on her face and put three out of five rounds in the board, from maybe ten feet away.

Billy went to take the revolver from her to reload it, but she said, "Let me. Show me."

I said, "First you got to dump the empties. Flip open that little gate on the right side. Put her on half-cock and turn the cylinder and shake 'em out. If they don't drop clear, there's an extractor rod and spring under the barrel to push 'em out."

Five seconds later she was empty and Billy handed her five fresh rounds.

"Do the same thing?" she asked.

"Nope," I said. "This time put two rounds in the top half of the board, then two in the bottom, then back to the top."

"Like I was shooting at different people?"

"Yes, ma'am."

"It's so loud. It makes my ears ring."

"It does, Emmalee. But remember that the muzzle blast is more startling to the folks you're shooting at than it is to you. Go ahead on, now. You're shooting good."

"But I missed twice."

"Not by much. Go ahead."

She put all five rounds in the board, just the way I told her to. The look on her face was pure joy. She dumped the empties and said, "I hope that's enough. I can hardly hear you talk."

"It's enough. You're a natural shooter. Billy will show you how to clean it, but first I want to walk you through a regular reload. For normal carry, I mean."

"It's different from how I did it?"

"It is. It ain't smart to carry a revolver full-loaded. You want a empty chamber under the hammer, so's it don't get bumped and go off accidental. What you do is to load one chamber, skip one, then load the next three. That'll put your hammer resting on a empty chamber."

"But I'll only have four bullets."

"Exactly. I carry six-shooters but only have five rounds loaded. Cowpunchers and Rangers often keep a dollar bill or maybe a sawbuck in that empty chamber. We'd say, 'Load one, pass the buck, load four more.' That buck would be emergency money. Liquor, women, such as that. For me, it's strictly funeral money."

"For who?"

"Me."

"Brodie, you are so funny. Now, what if you're expecting trouble? You still leave them loaded that way?"

I said, "Trouble don't normally give you much warning, but if you got time, well, then you don't pass the buck. Main thing, though, is if you got cause to expect trouble, you have yourself a repeating rifle or carbine. That's what you do your fighting with, even close up, if you can help it."

"But why?"

"They shoot straighter and harder, even with the same cartridges."

She said, "I don't understand."

"Well, your bullet flies truer and it builds up more speed in them longer barrels. Other thing is they're faster and easier to reload than revolvers. Here, I'll show you. Billy, go get that Yellowboy. You ought to have it with you, anyways. Anybody might come up on us sudden-like out here. And bring a box of cartridges."

He hung his head and said, "Sorry," and turned to go.

I said, "I was wasn't fussing at you, Billy. It's my fault, not teaching you that already. I should of thought of it, not you."

He smiled and took off running.

Emmalee patted my good arm and said, "You handled that

well. Maybe the marshal is right about you, after all."

I probably blushed my own self. I swear, she made me feel like a young boy, a durn unbroke colt.

I said, "Billy's gone for a minute. I got to ask you something. Byden said you was carrying a baby. Said he was worried you might lose it if, you know, if you was pushed hard or something . . ."

Durn, I felt stupid. I hadn't thought that question all the way through before I started asking it.

She stared at me. I realized I hadn't ever asked her nothing.

"Well, the thing is," I blundered on, "you sure don't look like you're about to have no baby. Did you, I mean, did they cause you . . ."

She patted my arm again and I stopped yammering.

"They did push me hard, and I was used hard, but not often and not for too long, thanks to you. And yes, I am carrying still. I can feel I've put on some weight, but I won't really show for another month or so. You are sweet to worry."

Sweet. Ain't nobody ever called me sweet before. I was so deep in trouble I couldn't see my way out. Didn't see how it could get no worse and then she leaned over and kissed me.

It was on my cheek, but it purely struck me dumb.

Billy come running up with that carbine then, which probably kept me from making a total fool of myself.

A half-hour later we had finished the shooting lesson and was walking up to the soddy when Byden and the marshal come pounding in.

"What's wrong, Marshal?" I was concerned as they weren't pushing any stock and their horses were all lathered up.

"Ain't nothing wrong with us. We heard gunfire, so we come on quick."

Now I felt bad again. I said, "My fault, Marshal. I wasn't

thinking. We was shooting up a target, is all. Me and Billy, that is."

I glanced over at Emmalee and she didn't flinch, but I'm sure I could read relief in her eyes. Byden didn't want her handling no guns, especially with me.

Billy figured out what was going on, I guess, as he nodded and then said, "Horses?"

Marshal Sentell said, "We found two of 'em and one mule along with maybe fifteen head of cattle. Left 'em maybe a mile back when we come a-running to the dance."

Byden snorted, "Which wasn't no dance at all, turns out. Young 'uns playing with guns, is all."

I hated him. I bit my tongue.

"It wasn't play, Pudding," Emmalee said.

"And what would you know? What the hell would you know, anyways? And don't call me that."

The marshal gave Byden a harsh look and said, "Probably enough said. Miz Bonnett, if your boys can ride bareback, maybe they could ride back with us to round up that stock and bring 'em in. Deputy, you and Billy hold the fort here with the womenfolk. We won't be long, I hope, but I worry someone else might of heard all that shooting."

And he gave me a right harsh look too.

CHAPTER TWENTY

I sent Billy to set up over by the remains of the horse shed and told him to watch west and north. I took the Schofields, the Long Tom, and the bandolier and set myself in the wagon, looking out to the south. I figured that if the preacher came at all, he'd come from that way, like we did.

The women waited in the soddy, at least for a little while. Next thing I knew here come Emmalee, a canteen in one hand and that little Colt in the other.

"Where'd you get that?" I asked her.

"From the well," she said. "The sand has settled in it now and the water came up clean."

I said, "I was talking about that pistol."

"Oh. From Billy. Conchita and I took him some water too and I asked him for it. I told him I was coming to wait with you. Conchita stayed there with him, so he gave her your pistol."

"Lot of good that'll do if she ain't ever handled one."

Emmalee said, "They'll be fine. He emptied it and was showing her how to use it as I left. You don't really think the preacher is coming here, though, do you."

It was a statement instead of a real question, and she was right.

"I don't know why, but I ain't worried about it. I figure that storm caught them square. Still, us doing all that shooting wont real bright, so we need to stay on our toes here, leastways 'til Curly Jack and Puddin' get back. With them and the Bonnett boys here, I don't think the preacher would come against us, even if he could find us."

"Please don't call him Pudding. He'll take it as you making fun of him, and he'll take it out on me."

"All right. I wouldn't let him hear me, anyways, but I'll stop it. Look, I figured out my standing here. I'm like a old man stuck on a young girl. This ain't gonna turn out well."

She said, "What do you mean?"

"It's a simple truth, Emmalee. The marshal gave me a talking-to last night. He says ain't no good gonna come from me being hung up on you."

She patted my bad arm. It didn't hurt none.

"You know he's right, Brodie. But we can be friends."

Friends. Heckfire, shit, and damnation. I wasn't so sure about that. Goldurn Curly Jack Sentell anyways.

He'd sort of sat me down for a big brother lesson the night before.

We was getting settled in under the wagon. Billy was already doing a soft snore and the marshal was laying out his lariat around us like he always did.

"I'll tell you a story," he said, "seeing as you need to hear it. Back in Sweetwater they was a old man, maybe sixty years of age, and he lost his durn mind over a fifteen-year-old girl."

"What's that got to do with me?" I said.

"Hang on, Brodie. Listen and learn. He made a small fortune as a buffalo runner. Made enough to build a saloon and sporting place, see. A durn gold mine, as it turned out. That darky cavalry out to Fort Elliott? He figured they oughta have their own place away from the white folks. Put in that sporting palace called the Ring Town Saloon, maybe two or three miles outside of town. There was this one girl, see, part Choctaw, part darky, and two parts white, and she come on to him. Her momma was one of the working girls."

I said, "And he fell for it?"

"Like a durn brick. I mean, this was one good-looking child. Kind of a bronze color, I'd say. Pooched out in the right places. Slow moving and sweet as molasses. Once they married, I asked the colonel out at the fort what in almighty hell would make the old man think she was interested in anything more than his stash."

I said, "What did he say?"

"Dementia, is what he said. Said it means being old-age bat-shit crazy. That is exactly what he said. And he said it was something you could see in somebody else, but not in your own self. Said he'd seen a dozen old friends laugh at other old men who'd fell like that, then soon as some pretty young thing come on to them, they'd swear this time it was different."

"I still don't see how this relates to me. Emmalee ain't come on to me."

"It's the same thing, Brodie. There can't be no happy ending. Not for you, anyways. You're a young man, but you show signs of dementia."

I said, "How did it end up with the old man?"

Sentell shook his head. "Not so good, Brodie. She commenced to hook up with young soldiers and passersby, didn't even try to hide it. He shot hisself after he couldn't drink hisself to death."

"What happened to her?"

"She run off with that colonel."

I sat there staring at my missing hand and feeling more and more sorry for myself. She must have sensed it.

She said, "I know. I'll go and dig out your claw and let's see if you can wear it now. Maybe that will perk you up."

She hopped down from the wagon and started to leave, but

stopped and shielded her eyes to peer south across the river.

"Oh, my God! Is that another sandstorm?"

I got my scope on it pretty quick. It was a kind of dust cloud all right, but it wasn't no wind causing it.

"That's cattle," I said. "A bunch of cattle, and they're starting to run. And straight this way too."

Emmalee grabbed the scope and said, "Oh, Lord, they are. They're coming straight at us. I've heard of stampedes. They'll run right over us, flatten everything, and everybody. We've got to tell everybody to . . ."

"Easy, girl. Easy. They smell water. Ain't no holding them back, but they won't go no further than the river. They're just coming for an overdue drink."

"Well, my gosh, that scared me. Brodie, I am certain that's more than any fifteen head."

"Lady," I shook my head, "You are durn sure right. I'd say three or four hundred head, at least. Could be more, back in that dust. That's somebody's herd."

By then we could hear and maybe feel the thunder of thousands of hooves pounding right at us. The other women came out of the soddy to stare too.

The marshal showed up about then with his stock posse, and it was all they could do to keep those few mounts and cattle from fleeing back downstream again.

I know you've seen that old bartender trick of putting a rattler in a dry pickle jar, and betting grown men they can't hold their hand against the glass when that durn snake strikes. Can't nobody do it. Ain't no way to do it.

This was something like that. I mean, I knew those cows was gonna stop at that river. That pissant little shallow river. I knew it. Still . . .

I told Emmalee and the others to go back in the soddy and brace the door. Had to yell to get through to them. Billy and

Conchita and Emmalee ignored me and climbed in the wagon with me.

The marshal, Byden, and the Bonnett brothers stayed mounted, and pulled in behind the wagon.

There won't a single durn throat there that didn't have a heart in it, watching maybe a hundred thousand pounds of meat and horns and hooves bearing down on us.

And then they stopped. Hit the river, milled about, and stopped. Not one crossed to our side. I started breathing again.

CHAPTER TWENTY-ONE

Emmalee sent Billy to fetch my claw, then helped me put it on. We's sitting there admiring all these critters, lining that river east and west and trying to drink it dry when five riders parted the herd and rode up to us. One tall older man and four young buckaroos, all toting about an inch of traildust.

"How do?" The old man croaked. "I'm Pitser Chisum, brother to John Chisum, and I'm moving my operations up here from the Pecos, to get away from them damn Lincoln county bandits. You folks ain't into cattle rustling, is you?"

Marshal Sentell said, "Me and young Claw there is lawmen. Both ex-Rangers. We ain't partial to thieves in general. Mister Byden here and most of the women is sheepherders . . ."

"Sheepherders?" Chisum spat.

"From over to Tascosa, Texas," the marshal continued. "Ain't nowhere near here. Won't bother you none. That there is Miz Bonnett. Her and her two boys own this spread. They got a few head of cows themselves. Damn few."

Chisum said, "Thankee, Marshal," then faced the old hag. "If me and the boys could swing down and visit your well, Miz Bonnett, I would then like to talk some business with you."

I'd never heard of no Pitser Chisum, but I'm pretty sure the only folks as didn't know of his brother locally must of lived under a durn rock. John Chisum was known as the Cattle King of the Pecos. His ranch was said to run a hundred miles along

101

the Pecos River, some distance west of the Llano Estacado.

That night, Pitser Chisum had his chuckwagon set up alongside the Bonnetts' cabin, and fed us under the stars. Over steak and beans, Chisum told us his brother got fed up and sold out.

"The good days might be over. Oliver Loving's been dead more'n ten years, Charlie Goodnight has gone to Colorado, and my brother has done give up. Let me have the cream off his herd afore he sold it, which is what you see here. Fine stock. Brother John is backing some new man for marshal, name of Garrett. Hopes he'll clean up the rustlers so's we can go back."

The marshal said, "Pat Garrett? About six foot fourteen inches?"

"Maybe not that high, but he's pretty tall," Chisum smiled. "Anyways, I just worked a deal with the Bonnetts here. Gonna make this my headquarters and free-graze my herd north of the river. She'll work with my cook and I'll employ her sons and provide all the food. Rebuild her barn and shed. Set up a corral, put us up a bunkhouse and line camps. Kill any sumbitch or Injin as looks sideways at my beef."

I said, "I don't suppose you come across any band of scoundrels led by a make-believe preacher in your travel toward here?"

"In fact, we did," Chisum said. "Couple days' south. Said they was bound for Wichita Falls and got blown south by a sandstorm. Lost a man, couple of mounts, and their pack mules. Had a couple riding double and was pretty near the end of their rope."

"I don't guess you found cause to hang 'em," Sentell said.

"Not right off. I sold 'em two mounts and give 'em a lame heifer. They snuck back in and took a few more head the next evening."

"That's Preacher Vance and his gang," the marshal said.

"They killed my woman over to Sweetwater, took these women prisoner. We took 'em back and killed Preacher's brother in the process. Now they's chasing us."

"Hunter's done become the hunted. Funny. That Preacher feller said he was chasing two make-believe lawmen with some stolen whores. My apologies, ladies."

"You put any stock in that?" the marshal put one hand on a pistol, so I did too.

"Not ary bit," Chisum snorted. "Man don't get to my advanced state out here if he ain't some kind of a judge of character. I weren't too surprised when they stole from us. Only wisht I'd had enough men to go after 'em. I see 'em again, they're dead."

"Any chance they followed you here?"

"Nossir. You see my man there in the sombrero? That's Injun Bob, my half-Mex tracker. I sent him to follow 'em a ways, make sure they wasn't trailing us for more rustling. They went south and east. He fired on 'em from a distance to speed 'em along."

The marshal said, "Good man."

Chisum said, "Yep, he is that. Looks like maybe they was cutting more toward Wichita Falls or even Fort Richardson or Fort Worth, 'stead of Tascosa or Sweetwater."

The marshal said, "Well, good. Ain't likely they'll give up on us, though. Anyways, I don't mean to wait for 'em. Soon as we gets these folks home to Tascosa, we're going after the preacher ourselves. Turn this thing around again."

Chisum shifted to look at me. "You up to that, you think, with your hook and all?"

There was still some daylight left. I picked up my carbine and aimed at a lone buzzard sailing in circles, looking for dead livestock from that storm. I didn't hit it, but I did cause it to change directions.

"Damn!" Chisum said.

"Not bad for a short-handed man, huh? Leastways I scared it."

"That wont what I was cursing about, boy. It's a wonder you didn't startle my whole durn herd into running again."

Marshal Sentell stood up and fixed me with that glare of his. "You simply ain't right, Brodie. How'd you like to be out chasing steers all night? Didn't I say enough about gunfire today already?"

I tried to slink off underneath a rock, but Old Man Chisum pulled me back.

"Lemme look at that hook contraption."

I did. Seemed the least I could do to calm him and his durn herd down.

"Right nice," he said. "You can pick up stuff, aim a carbine with it. Who made it?"

Billy was about to nod off again, having recovered from my gunshot. I pointed to him.

"Whyn't you stay here and go to work for me?" Chisum asked Billy. "I can surely use somebody who can come up with a dang thing like that."

Billy looked totally confused.

The marshal stood and walked to where Billy sat beside the fire. He rubbed Billy's neck and said, "Billy sort of rides with me. His momma was my woman. Still and all, I'll run over this with him tonight, make sure he knows this here is a actual job offer. How much?"

"Thirty a month and found, same as my other hands," Chisum said. He didn't flinch, and he knew durn well Billy was a real youngster. And couldn't talk good.

Billy said, "Found what?"

The marshal said softly, "It means your food, Billy. It's a good offer. C'mon, now, let's get you down. We'll talk on this."

Billy and the marshal headed off toward Byden's wagon. I hung on a minute or two.

"That his daddy?"

"Nossir, Mister Chisum, but he might as well be."

"You think the marshal will talk him out of staying? I wont making no joke about putting that boy to work."

Chisum pulled a flask and took a hit on it. He didn't offer me none. Could be he was worried about me firing off another gun.

"Nossir," I said again. "The marshal truly looks out for the boy's interests. I don't think it really matters none. That boy is head over heels in love with that little deaf girl, Conchita."

"Hellfire, Brodie, I'll hire her too. Half-wages to cook, sew, whatever, anything to keep that boy here."

I shook my head. "I ain't sure, of course, but I 'spect she'll go with her momma."

"And Billy will follow along," he said.

"Yessir," I said, "A dollar against a buffalo chip says he will."

"Well, you tell him and the marshal what I said about the deaf girl. Let him decide. They stir up a baby between 'em, he'll be looking for a job. And maybe looking to stay away from her daddy."

I said goodnight and went to the wagon. Told Billy and the marshal what-all Mister Chisum had said, but it didn't change a thing. I didn't think it would.

"Get some sleep, Brodie. I mean to get our Tascosa gang moving again come morning, now that I see you can handle that carbine all right."

I said, "I guess Byden's in a rush to get home."

"I ain't so worried about that as I am about you starting a goldurn stampede."

CHAPTER TWENTY-TWO

We almost made it out of that cow camp clean.

See, most of Mister Chisum's cowpunchers was teenage boys. Tough as nails, but by and large they was shy. Scared of most women but especially pretty ones.

Still, though, there was one older rowdy in Chisum's crew that was determined to show his younger trail-buddies what a stud horse he was. Maybe thirty years old and well fed, least-ways for a New Mexico wrangler.

He caught Emmalee coming from the privy and made a rude comment that I won't repeat. Me and three of the young cowboys was nearby. One giggled, one laughed, one muttered "Butt-head," and Emmalee got all red-faced.

I had a Schofield in my belt, so I drew and covered the scoundrel. When he heard the "click-clack" of that revolver locking up he froze first and then turned to me right slow-like.

"Say you're sorry," I said, "Or say goodbye."

"I ain't holding," he said.

"Well, that makes you stupid and rude. I ain't heard that apology."

He said, "You'd shoot an unarmed man? Whyn't you put that hogleg down and let's fight."

He had me by thirty pounds and six inches in height and reach. And one hand.

I said, "Here's what I'll do. I'll shoot off your left hand and then we'll go at it."

I pointed that Smith and Wesson at his hand and he jerked it around behind him.

"Whoa!" he said.

"If I shoot your hand right now, I'm gonna ruin your belly and back end," I said. "Whyn't you hold it out to the side?"

The marshal had come up by then. He must of asked somebody what happened, because he took his rifle and slammed that trash-talker in the side of his head with the butt-end. Big Mouth folded like a empty potato sack.

"I had it under control, Curly," I said.

"Naw, you didn't, either, Brodie. You was about to fire off another gun, maybe start a stampede and get us hung by these cowpokes."

Pitser Chisum walked up at that point and asked what happened. After the marshal told him, he stopped a cowpoke riding out to the herd and took his canteen. Took about half that cold water to bring Big Mouth around.

When he sat up, Chisum said, "Listen up, Jerkwad, you're a fair bronc buster, but not good enough for me to tolerate no such talk to no married woman. You want to go apologize now, or pack your gear and ride?"

Big Mouth was kind of cross-eyed from that lick Curly gave him. He said, "I'm truly sorry, Mister Chisum."

"Look at me if you're gonna talk to me, you wall-eyed dumbass. Now take your butt over to Byden's wagon and speak your 'sorrys' to Miz Byden. And if Mister Byden chooses to whip your butt sixteen ways from Sunday, don't be looking for no help."

He stopped and glared around. "Leastways not from nobody who aims to work for me tomorrow."

An hour later we were crossing the river and cutting east for Tascosa.

★ ★ ★ ★ ★

Marshal Sentell had me ride point, a half mile to a mile out front of the wagon. That was a good thing for more than one reason.

It kept me and Byden apart for most of the time. I guess that was most important, but then, who else was gonna do it? The marshal needed to be with the main group as there wasn't no promise a problem would only come from up front. Byden durn sure couldn't take the point, nor Billy.

Still, it made me feel good that the marshal trusted me with the job. Being out front and alone gave me some time to practice using my scope and drawing and aiming my carbine. I did fumble some at first but didn't actual drop nothing and by evening of that first day's ride, I'd gotten right smooth.

Not cocky, exactly, but a durn site more comfortable of my prospects if we got in another gunfight. Which did seem likely.

Other reason the job was timely was it helped keep my mind off Emmalee. Out on point, I had to keep studying every bush and patch of trees, every gully and ridgeline. Preacher could have been most anywhere.

I must of jumped up five pronghorns that day along with several big nervous turkeys. Every durn one of them put my heart in my gullet and seized up my butt, tight as Dick's hatband. Nervous? Them turkeys didn't hold a candle to me.

As it come near dusk I found us a little stand of cottonwoods on a creek that had a actual trickle in it. Pretty good spot to spend the night. I rode a circle around it, maybe a half mile out, even crossed and recrossed the river, then headed back to bring the others to it.

It was good to be off the point and heading for some conversation, vittles, and the sight of Emmalee. I was so relaxed I nearly rode over the man in the bushes.

CHAPTER TWENTY-THREE

If I was startled, he was terrified. In the half-hour or so since I'd passed by there, he'd started to set up camp along my back-trail.

He came strolling out of them bushes, trying to button his pants. Hadn't even pulled up his suspenders yet. His mare was snorting and stomping, which might be why he didn't hear me ride up. Probably caused him to rush his business. He said something like, "Easy, girl, you hear something?"

When I rode into that clearing, he was twenty feet from his hardware, which was a Sharps carbine and a belt pistol hanging on his saddle. He glanced at his guns as I drew and cocked a Schofield, which froze him.

"Easy now," I said. "Put them hands up."

"I do and my breeches'll fall down," he said. "Can I just put one up?"

"That'll do for now. You trailing me?"

"I ain't trailing nobody, son. Don't you reckon I'da taken my revolver with me to do my business, was I tracking somebody? Jesus, it's a good thing my bowels are empty. You woulda scared the mess outa me."

"What you doing here, if you ain't trailing me?" I still wasn't buying his story.

"I come north, heading for Colorado territory. I hope you ain't bent on robbing me. Some wayward reverend and his gang robbed me yesterday. I ain't got jack-squat left but guns, bullets, and beans."

I said, "You sure they ain't chasing you?"

"Why would they? Done took my pack mule and all my goods. I had to leave 'em and ride like a bandit to get clear of 'em, but when I pulled up on a ridge and glassed 'em, they was heading off down my backtrail. Can I fix my breeches now?"

"Go ahead," I said. "But stay away from them guns. Where you coming from?"

"I was working a spread down low in the Panhandle. Some durn foreigners bought it and cut me loose. Too old, they said. I'm hoping this here is the Canadian River."

"It is."

"Well, my plan is to follow it back up to Raton and Trinidad. See can I find work."

I said, "You might find work across the river and a day's ride west. A Mister Chisum has brought up a herd from the Pecos and set up camp there."

He said, "Obliged. Where you heading?"

"I'm riding point for some durn sheepherders going back to their camp at Tascosa, on down the Canadian. Right now I'm heading back to lead 'em into night camp, maybe a mile back east. They's following me slow. Wagon, women, and all."

"Well, son, I hope you won't shoot me as you pass back by here. I ain't got much, but I'll share what I have to eat."

"Maybe we'll take you up on that," I said. I didn't tell him we was rich compared to him. After his kindly offer, I figured we'd surprise him. He looked hungry.

When we came back by the stranger's camp, it consisted of his horse hobbled, his saddle over a log, and small fire going. Didn't take much to convince him to join us for the night.

We all went on to the site I'd picked. We fed him good and he told the story of being robbed by the preacher, and how the gang had rid off away from us. I think we all slept better that night and we parted ways at dawn.

Next few days we made good time, free of excitement, though I hardly got to speak with Emmalee. Byden had her on a short rope, so to speak. Only hope I found was that him and Emmalee didn't seem to be hitting it off so good themselves. I heard harsh words a few times between them but couldn't make out exactly what was said.

Anyways, you never seen such a hullabaloo as when we got back to Tascosa. We had more roast lamb, lamb stew, fried lamb, peppers, and beans than we could handle.

Turns out Conchita's momma lived with the blacksmith, and he was even more interested in my claw hand and how Billy had come up with it than most folks was.

Didn't seem at all bothered that his stepdaughter was sweet on Billy. Matter of fact, it was more the other way. He asked Billy to stay on and work with him. I don't think Billy studied on that more than five seconds before he said yes. He didn't even look at the marshal.

"You gonna let him stay here, Marshal?"

"He ain't mine, Brodie. I got no say in it, unless he asks me. And come to think of it, it ain't such a bad idea."

I said, "How come?"

"He can shoot. You let him keep your carbine and Colt, and I'll replace 'em with new ones, once we're back in Sweetwater. This place is growing hand over foot, what with big cattle ranches coming in. Got a saloon and a store under roof since we left. Folks here might need him and them guns."

"Yeah, Marshal, but how's he gonna get along? I mean, language and all."

"Shoot, Brodie, the blacksmith hisself is a white man. He speaks more Mex than Billy speaks English. And them two lovebirds seem to get across to each other just fine."

"Maybe I should stay on too. Watch over him a while."

"Nosir, Brodie. Nossiree. You got no business here. Besides, them banditos is gonna come for us, sooner or later, and they'll look for us in Sweetwater. Preacher will want us dead and gone before they come snooping around Tascosa again."

I was trying to think up a better reason to stay, but the marshal didn't let up.

"Anyways, Deputy, I don't mean to wait for 'em. I need to clean things up in town, set up another deputy, maybe, and then you and me is going manhunting. You up for that, or did you really wanna hang out here, staring at something you can't have? You know, maybe working your way up to Deputy Sheepherder or something like that?"

Shoot. He was right again. Seems like he was always right.

Chapter Twenty-Four

Despite that Panhandle wind, it was pretty nice to get back to Sweetwater. The marshal got us both paid straight away, and Godiva Jones chased off the bull-whacker she'd took up with in my absence, so I settled back in with her.

The marshal found me in her room on the third morning home.

"Town leaders weren't too happy with me being gone so long," he said. "They are pleased we killed three of the banditos, but don't want to spend nothing on us chasing Preacher Vance no more."

I said, "So, you gonna let it go and hang around here? Sorta wait for 'em?" I knew better than that.

"Hell, Brodie, you know better than that. We got a little jingle in our pockets and we know about where they was heading. I say we load up and go right at 'em."

"I got no long gun, Marshal. You gave my perfectly good carbine to Billy. And my matching Colt." They wasn't really a matched pair, but he knew what I meant. They both shot forty-four Henry Flats.

"I know what you mean," he said. "Drag your lazy butt up and I'll show you something. Godiva, help him into them trousers."

"Let him help hisself," she said. "I got to run catch somebody."

"Who?"

"That durn bullwhacker. He ain't as pretty as Deputy Dent here, but he's sturdy. And he don't ever go chasing bandits." She always seen things pretty clear.

We got me dressed and went over to the old Rath and Hanrahan store. Sentell nodded to the proprietor and the man pulled out a heavy long-barreled revolver with a bird's-head grip. Put it on the counter and pushed it at me.

I said, "I've seen some small ones like that. It's a Colt, right?"

He said, "Yep. It's called the Double Action Frontier Model. It's a self-cocker." He set a box of cartridges on the counter by it. Winchester cartridges.

It took a second for it to sink in. "Whoa," I said. "You mean it'll handle forty-four forty rifle cartridges?"

"Yes it will, Brodie. It ain't a top-break like the Schofield, so's you can't load and unload it easy as them, but you can shoot it double- or single-action. Colt has come up with a companion for the '73 Winchester. Go ahead, Jake. Give him the carbine too."

It was a brand new Winchester carbine.

This was something we'd been pulling for, for over five years. The 1873 Winchester was a stronger gun than my '66 model and used a more powerful cartridge, the Forty-Four Winchester Central Fire. The slug was pushed by forty grains of powder so it was known as "The Forty-Four Forty." The rimfire cartridge for the Henry and '66 model only had maybe twenty-five grains of powder.

The 1873 Colt was a great belt pistol but until now was only in forty-five Colt caliber, and Schofields used shorter forty-five Schofield shells. Good cartridges, but there wasn't no carbines or rifles in either size. Now we had a pistol, carbine, and cartridge combination that was about as good as it gets.

"How much?" I said. "For both, I mean."

The man nodded toward the marshal and said, "All paid up.

Three boxes of shells too. This as well." He held up a gunbelt with a crossdraw holster for the Frontier and plenty of cartridge loops. Nothing new there, but it was set up with wide canvas suspenders, and a easy hook in front.

"Oughta be easier for you to get into," the marshal said. "And out of. I can't always be there to dress you like a durn baby." He was grinning like a cat with two dead mice. "I got you two more of them Frontier Models for your pommel holsters."

I tried to talk, to ask why, but couldn't. Must of been something caught in my throat.

"Why, you might ask?" Durn old mind reader. "Well, Deputy, I missed my Schofields. And now you're all in one caliber. No way to mess up a reload, even an idjit like you."

We set out south the next morning.

The marshal allowed we'd cross the North and Salt forks of the Red and keep bearing due south until we hit the Prairie Dog Fork. We could follow it east to the Red and then on down it to the Wichita River and down to the Falls.

Figured we'd find them there or maybe learn where they were.

The ride wasn't too bad, but summer was over and that wind had a little bite to it. We had to pull our scarves up over our hats to keep them on. Several mornings out we had hit the Red and had to break out our slickers as that wind picked up and come at us out of the northeast, right into our faces.

That wind maybe saved us.

CHAPTER TWENTY-FIVE

We had got off to a good early start, but we did have coffee and bacon and biscuits and honey first, and all those wonderful smells was blown away off into the prairie behind us.

Wasn't even a quarter hour later that same wind blew some of them same tasty scents into our faces, along with mesquite smoke.

"Coming out of that draw, off a shade to the left, some closer to the river. You mark it?" The marshal's whisper sounded like a durn steam engine to me, but I guess that wind saved us again.

I said, "Well, I ain't dead. I reckon I do."

He grinned and said, "Let's tie off here and ease up on 'em. Could be LT ranch cowpokes, but could be our Preacher and his boys."

I dismounted, pulled my carbine and checked the chamber, leaving it on half-cock. Curly Jack did too, but then he shucked his slicker and put on a canvas belt of shotgun shells from the pack mule and grabbed that sawed-off ten-gauge double he liked for town work.

I come out of my slicker too and got an immediate chill, which I don't think had a durn thing to do with the weather.

We eased over to the lip of that gully, laid down, and gazed down on a right messy little cow camp. Six horses, maybe twenty head of cattle grazing in the flat along the river. Bedrolls and ground sheets was strewn from hell to Christmas along with saddles and slickers.

Four cowpunchers setting around a blazing fire, having themselves a fine city breakfast. By that I mean relaxed and unarmed. I could plainly count four gunbelts and four carbines up against their saddles.

The marshal had his scope on them. "I can make out the LT brand on most of them cattle, but I don't believe these boys is from the LT spread."

I whispered, "Why?" I mean, all cowpokes looked the same to me, and these boys sure didn't seem like they was a band of tight-wired rustlers, having themselves a late-morning meal. Heckfire, it had to be going on seven o'clock. For durn sure, wont none of them the preacher.

The marshal said, "All the LT boys carry rolling-block carbines. L.T. hisself issued 'em. Most of 'em pack Remington revolvers too, to use the same forty-six rimfire cartridges. I don't see a single Remington down there. Do you?" He handed me his scope.

He was right. He was always right. I shook my head and handed back the scope.

He said, "Could be they ain't bandits, but we'll treat 'em as such. I think that's a running iron in the fire."

He laid the scope by his Winchester, cocked that shotgun, and stood up. I struggled to my feet too, got my carbine into my claw, and cocked it. And moved several steps away from the marshal. Didn't want to give them an easy shot, in case they had a shotgun amongst themselves.

"Morning, boys," he yelled. "Y'all kind of hold what you got 'til we sort out who is who here."

Three of them froze. One stood and yelled back, "Who in the hell are you?"

The marshal said, "I'm a marshal. That there is my deputy. And if you're law-abiding, God-fearing citizens, you got nothing to fear from us, neither one."

We scrambled down the side of the gully and got closer.

Curly squinted at the cattle like he was first noticing them. "LT brand. I guess you boys work for old Larry Thomas over west of here."

"Yessir, Marshal, we sure do." Their talker looked around at the others. "Don't we, boys?"

They all nodded. I swear I could see sweat on one's bald head. See, the problem was that everbody in the Panhandle knew that Lew Turner owned the LT spread.

Curly said, "Manny Ramirez still his number two?"

"He is, Marshal. Manny is still the Segundo. Now, can we get our stuff together and start pushing these steers west again?"

Manny Ramirez was a former highwayman that Curly had put out of business a year ago. With that same shotgun he was holding steady on these boys.

So, we'd found some bandits, but not the ones we wanted.

Curly said, "No, son, that ain't gonna happen. I need you to get back on the ground. Set yourself down."

The bandit said, "That ain't gonna happen, either," and made a dive for his carbine.

I shot him in midair and shucked in another round, smooth as silk. I was right proud of that shot, nervous as I was.

It hit him in the hip and knocked him sideways, away from his guns and saddle. The marshal moved left a little and gave him a blast of buckshot when he tried to sit up. Blew up dust and dirt all around that fool.

The other three jumped a little, then froze again.

"Here's the thing, boys. The only question now is do I shoot you, hang you, or have you push this beef back to the LT spread. It belongs to Lew Turner. And Manny Ramirez is long dead, bless his thieving heart. You boys lay on your bellies. Spread eagle. Pronto!"

They did.

"Cover 'em, Deputy, while I reload."

I did.

"Now take one of 'em and go bring in our mounts. Don't let him near my carbine, and don't leave it lying there, neither."

I did that too. Curly Jack Sentell was one easy man to work for, so long as you did exactly what he told you.

CHAPTER TWENTY-SIX

Time we got back down in their camp, Curly already had the other two with their durn hands tied in front.

"How'd you swing that, Marshal?"

He said, "I had the boy tie the bald one, then I tied him. You got my scope?"

I handed it over. "You gonna tie this one too, or can I go on and shoot him?" I didn't really want to kill the boy. He weren't no more than a scared teenager, but I did want him to stay scared.

"See can you tie him, Brodie. You got to learn knots with your dang hook sometime."

I did that too. I was thinking that Emmalee would of been proud, when that boy interrupted my thoughts.

"It's too tight," he said.

"And you were standing there thinking I was trying to make you comfortable? Marshal, it's better than a day's ride to the LT spread even if we wasn't pushing cattle. I say we hang 'em and let the durn cows find their own way home."

I gave Curly a wink as I stood up. He nodded.

He said, "Now, take it easy, Brodie. I know you want to hang these boys 'cause of them rustlers shooting off your hand. Thing is, though, we might need them to help us move these steers home."

The older bald bandit said, "You two are the ones that Preacher feller is hunting for. I just figgered it out."

I said, "Where'd you see him?"

"We can cut a deal here. I can tell you where we seen him and where he is now."

Curly walked over and stood over him. "So, I let you go and you'll tell me?"

"Hell, Mister, you let me go and I'll take you to him. I'll help you kill him. I'm serious."

Curly cocked that shotgun. "Here's a better thought. You tell me and I don't shoot off this foot." He kicked the man's left foot. "See, I can find him myself. All I need is for you to tell me where he's heading."

The man sagged like a limp drunk. "You'd do it, wouldn't you? You ain't no better than me. All right. We seen 'em in Wichita Falls. They was heading for Jacksboro first, then Weatherford."

"Well, thank you," Curly said. "You can hang on to that foot a while."

By midmorning, we were heading west, down our own backtrail. We had lashed those rustlers' feet together under their horses' bellies, and their hands was still tied in front. And Curly had told them I was dying to kill them, so we didn't have any trouble at all. They was the most willing cowpokes I ever seen.

Once we had them cattle well on to the LT range, Curly said, "Y'all go on now. Ride for your lives. I'd go south, if I was you."

The bald one said, "You ain't gonna cut us loose?"

Curly said, "I am cutting you loose, but I ain't cutting your ropes. Deputy, hang a canteen on one of them saddle horns. And if I ever sees any of you boys again, anywheres but inside a church, I mean to shoot you."

The bald one said, "It ain't right, us with no guns, nor food nor bedrolls. And tied, to beat that. I'm telling you this ain't no way to treat a fellow man. Ain't you got a Christian bone in your body?"

I don't think that old boy was too bright, arguing with a impatient mankiller like the marshal. Probably should of chose a different line of work. Lawyering, maybe.

I said, "Marshal, let me cut that one out and hang him, if you're so all-fired set to let the young ones go."

As impatient as he was to get after our own banditos, the marshal was still more tolerant than me.

"It ain't like they stole horses, Brodie. It ain't but a few cattle." He turned back to Baldy. "You want to ride back to your camp and pick up them bedrolls after we pass, have at it. I mean to sell your guns and pack horses in Wichita Falls. I expect me and my deputy will share your coffee and sugar and eat your grub."

Baldy sputtered and stammered some more, but then gave up and they headed south. That little bit of arguing was no more than spitting upwind, and it might have been the difference between living and dying for them.

I said, "You done right, Curly. You know I didn't want to hang them kids, not really. Even Baldy wasn't yet thirty."

Curly Jack nodded then jerked a thumb toward the west. "Maybe so, Brodie, but it don't make no nevermind. If that ain't Lew Turner on that white horse, I'll eat my hat."

He didn't have to eat his hat. The LT ranch owner and five of his hands was bearing down hard on us. When they come inside a hundred yards, Curly raised his hat and opened his coat. Could of been his bald head or the flash of that tin badge on Curly's vest, but anyways the man on the white stallion jabbed a finger at the cow thieves and his hands veered off to run them down, while he rode right up to us.

As the cow man slowed to a walk and patted that stallion's neck, Curly said, "Lew."

The rancher nodded. "Captain. Long time. Your man?"

Curly said, "He is. Brodie Dent, meet Lew Turner."

Turner pulled off his hat and swabbed his forehead with a shirt sleeve. His hair was thick and as white as his horse, and he was a tall, hard man.

"You still a Ranger, Captain Sentell?"

"Nosir. A marshal, out of Sweetwater these days. We's after some different bandits when we stumbled on these, a few miles downriver."

"Were you releasing those men? Or did they bolt when they saw us?" The old man jammed his hat back in place.

"I was releasing 'em, Lew. I got no jurisdiction here. I did kill their leader. Only brought them boys back this far to help us herd your cows home."

"You're getting soft, Captain. Still, you saved us some hard riding. One of my line riders saw them pushing these steers east and came for help."

Soft? Curly Jack Sentell soft? I thought, if he thinks Curly is soft, these boys we cut loose might certainly be in deep water.

His men brought in the three bandits about then. You never seen such a hangdog pair as the two young ones. The bald one had got more stupid, if you can believe that.

"Listen here. You can't do nothing to us. We done been freed by the law. Tell him, Marshal. He's got no rights, has he?" He was missing his hat.

A big Mex vaquero said, "The hairless one, *mi coronel?* Him, I have seen before, and he's riding one of our *caballos.* See? The LT brand is now a top hat."

Lew Turner rode close to Baldy and squinted at the brand. "That's no fresh burn, either. You've been riding a stolen horse for some time, haven't you, boy?"

Baldy said, "Well, it ain't my mount. It belonged to our boss, but that lawman gunned him down. My horse was kind of weak, so . . ."

Lew Turner drew a big nickel-plated Remington and shot the

man, mid-sentence. And mid-body. Baldy made a whoofing sound, and that slug knocked him sideways. He would of hit the ground but his wrist rope was over the saddle horn and his feet was still tied so he sort of slumped off the side with his butt hanging down.

And he wasn't dead. Him jerking and twitching and being off that Appaloosa's right side didn't set well with the horse, so he went to bucking.

Lew Turner yelled, "Dammit to hell, Hernando, get a rope on that bronc. Then take all three of the scoundrels to a big cottonwood and hang them." He turned to us and smiled.

"Now, how about a bite to eat and a drink of whiskey, Captain?"

He was what you needed to be to run a large ranch, I guess. Not soft. Not one durn bit.

The big Mex rode up then. He'd roped Baldy's mount and shoved him back in the saddle.

"*Jefe,* you see this one? He ain't gonna make it through no hanging. You shot him good."

"Well, hang him fast, then, Segundo. I want them all hung, dead or alive. And leave them hanging. But wait a minute. Captain Sentell, did you bury their leader?"

Curly said, "Well, a little. We was kind of crimped for time."

Turner said, "Good. Segundo, send a man with a spade to find that camp and bring their leader back here. Hang him too."

Jumping Jehosaphat Christmas.

CHAPTER TWENTY-SEVEN

We were finishing our beans and whiskey and coffee when Turner's big Number Two rode up again, this time with a scrawny teenager pulling a mule.

"*Jefe,* I am sending Squeak now to find that dead bandito, but I don't know how far it is, and he don't have no shovel."

Turner stood and turned to Curly. "I see you have a spade on your pack mule. I'm sure you and your deputy want to get moving, so why don't you show Squeak the way? Perhaps let him use your tool once you're there?"

"It's near dark, Lew, and a half-day's ride from here. We'll take him, camp along the way and then hook him up with the body come morning. He should be back here mid-afternoon."

"Fine. Segundo, leave someone here to help him hang the last one once he's back. I've got to head back to the ranch come dawn. Squeak, don't dawdle. Sentell, visit when you can."

We were dismissed. We saddled up and rode off east again as it turned to a cool dusk. A couple of miles out I said, "Why'd he call you 'Captain' back there?"

"He was my colonel during the war. Made me a captain and a troop commander toward the end. Fourteen years later, he still likes to call me 'Captain' to keep me mindful of my place."

"I notice you didn't call him 'Colonel.' In fact, you called him his first name."

Curly smiled. "I'm trying to learn him his place."

Squeak laughed. "Good luck with that."

He was a good kid, no more than sixteen, and he relaxed a lot once Lew Turner had disappeared behind us. Told us some tales that raised the hair on my neck, though Curly didn't seem so surprised.

"Used the lash in the olden days," Squeak said. "Like the marshal said, he thinks he's still a durn Confederate colonel or something. Shoot, I bet he whipped his slaves. If it wont for Hernando, the foreman, wouldn't nobody in their right mind work there. I mean, I seen him catch a old Tonk Injun eating one of his steers. He hung him, then cut off his head and stuck it on a fencepost."

"He didn't have no slaves," Sentell said. "He was a dog-assed poor lawyer, scrambling to eat before the war. Told folks he had army experience in Mexico back in the '48 war. He did, but only as a quartermaster. Fooled enough folks in our regiment that they made him colonel."

"Hard to believe there weren't no better men there fit to be colonel," I said.

Curly said, "There was. They led charges, which good cavalry leaders do, and they all was killed or crippled."

Squeak said, "Well, he weren't. Durn it all."

Curly said, "He wasn't about leading no charges. Sort of did his leading from behind."

"How'd he get so rich?" I asked.

"He come home a self-declared hero and found hisself a rich widow. Same one as owned this spread before he wed her and named the place after hisself."

Squeak said, "That's how I heard it, too. Anyways, I always got my eyes out for a rich widder woman myself."

Curly laughed. "Might want to get yourself made a colonel first. Let's stop and get some shut-eye."

★ ★ ★ ★ ★

We found the camp and dug up the bandit leader by midmorning. Rolled him in one of the abandoned ground sheets, and sent Squeak on his way before noon.

He yelled over his shoulder, "Y'all ever get a spread and look for help, lemme know. Y'all are easy to work with. Not like somebody I know."

In Wichita Falls we went straight to the livery. It was getting late.

"We'll stay at least one night," Curly told the owner. "That's our two horses and these two pack mules is ours too. Can you give me a price on them other three animals?"

"They ain't stolen, is they?"

Curly flashed his badge. "They belonged to a evil rustler who perished in front of my trusty shotgun. You interested, or do I need to go elsewhere? Maybe someplace with manners."

"Didn't mean no rudeness, Marshal. See, it ain't been a week since I bought two ponies off a durn preacher. Him and his Mex accomplice was riding the Bar-B brand so I figgered they was off that spread, down south of town. Turns out they murdered two Bar-B boys, swapped mounts with 'em, and sold me theirs."

"Did anybody catch this preacher?"

"Nosir. Leastways not yet. I'll work you up a price. How 'bout the tack?"

Curly said, "The whole kit. Now, whereabouts can we get some grub and a place to sleep?"

"They is a ass-burner of a Mex café two blocks down. Hotel is around the corner from that. They serve steaks. You can sleep there for a fee, or in the loft here for nothing."

We chose the hotel for food and beds.

Over steak and potatoes the marshal said, "Soon as we're

done eating, we'll look up the law here. See can we learn where Preacher headed from here."

"We gonna join the chase?"

Curly said, "Can't say. Depends on which way he fled, and what kind of posse took after him."

"Ain't all posse's pretty much the same?"

He said, "Naw, they ain't, not from a town this size. If they sent out fifteen married men, they'll run out of steam in three days, or as soon as they draw fire. Now, is they some Rangers mixed in, they'll likely keep pushing. Drive old Preacher all the way to Mexico. Or 'til they kill him."

I said, "So?"

"That being the case, a Ranger posse, Preacher's either gone for the winter, or he's a dead man waiting to happen. Either way, we can head home and wait there." He drained his beer and pushed back from the table.

I said, "I guess if they was all married and local, we'll stock up and keep chasing."

Curly said, "Yup. Right up to the gates of Hell. I don't care who kills him, I need to know he's dead. Brodie, you mark those two dirtbags over my left shoulder?"

"I do. What of 'em?"

"They been watching us. We'll keep an eye out for them. See do they follow us. Dang, I hate big towns. Always some scum looking to take advantage of a man's good nature."

They kept watching us as we paid and left, but they didn't follow us. Not as far as we could see.

CHAPTER TWENTY-EIGHT

The Wichita Falls marshal was cut from a different bolt of cloth than Curly Jack Sentell. To begin with, he was sitting in his office talking to us, 'stead of out leading that posse.

"Yeah," he said, "I sent out a few local men, but mostly they was cowpokes from the Bar-B spread. More'n I could pay too, and I tole 'em so."

Curly said, "Why'd they go? Revenge?"

"Could be that, I guess. They's about to be laid off for the winter, so maybe they wanted something to do. And them two was murdered? They was right well liked."

I said, "Any Rangers go with 'em?"

"I tole 'em we didn't need 'em," the hefty marshal said. "Think they's better'n everybody else in this business."

Curly said, "Yeah, but did they go?"

"A sergeant and two Rangers did," the so-called lawman muttered.

Curly said, "Good. Now, any chance they's a mercantile or gun store might buy some captured guns off us?"

"D.B. Jackson's Hardware Emporium is two blocks east. He trades in guns. You got many?"

Curly walked out without so much as a thank-you or goodbye.

Me too.

As we walked back to the hotel, Curly said, "It's such as him gives lawmen a bad name."

I said, "Well, Curly, you know there's a gracious plenty of lawmen who works both sides of the law."

He snorted, "I do know that, Brodie. I believe it was me as pointed that out to you. Anyways, I despise them. They's worse than common bandits. That fat ol' fart back there, though, he wouldn't even make a pimple on a good bandit's butt. Setting there at a desk, drawing pay as a marshal, letting his deputies do the job. And take the risk."

"Yessir. Now what's our plan?"

He said, "Get some shut-eye. Come dawn, we'll sell off them bandit guns and get paid for them horses. Provision up and head home."

I said, "Curly, ain't that the emporium there? Looks to be still open. All lit up."

He said, "Let's see can we move them guns tonight. You go ask 'em to stay open another half hour, and I'll go get the guns. Ain't but one hideaway, four belt guns, and four carbines. I can carry that many."

He walked off in the dark.

An hour later we headed for the hotel once more, eighty dollars better than we was before supper.

"They wouldn't buy the hideaway gun?"

"Fact is, Brodie, they would of. But I kind of like it." He had it palmed to show me how it hid complete inside his big fist. "It's a Remington two-shooter. Forty-one rimfire."

About then, two men stepped out of the dark of an alley, right in front of us. Those two dirtbags from the hotel café, only now they was sporting shiny badges.

"Well, if it ain't the old lawdog," the scrawny one sort of cackled. "And his sidekick, Claw-Boy."

"Yeah, and his sidekick, little Claw-Boy." That was the second one. I made him out to be about as deep in stupid as one can get.

Curly had left his shotgun in the room when he went back to pick up them other guns, but I had my new carbine down along my right leg. I thumbed the hammer back.

Curly said, "Step aside, else I'll rip off them badges and feed 'em to you. You ain't real lawmen, no more'n your town marshal."

Scrawny stepped back, but said, "Don't go for them sidearms. You ain't supposed to be carrying them in our town."

I don't think they saw my carbine. Neither one of them had drawn, but their right hands was resting on their gun butts.

"Yeah," said Stupid. "Not in our town."

Curly said, "We just come from the Marshal's office, and he didn't say no such thing."

Scrawny said, "Well, Mister Know-It-All Lawdog, the marshal is who sent us. Said you was carrying plenty of jingle now to pay your fine."

Stupid said, "Yeah, Mister Know-It-All Law, uh . . ."

Curly brought that little Remington up as he cocked it, and said, "Try this."

He shot each of them once, then dropped it and went for his Colt.

Wasn't no need. I drilled both of them again as they staggered back. That Winchester was smooth as silk. And fast. They both went flat on their backs.

Stupid jerked a little, so Curly shot him again. Whole shooting match didn't take four seconds.

Curly said, "Pull their hoglegs and lay them by their hands. I'll grab them badges. Hurry, afore a crowd shows. And fire off one round from each of their guns."

I did precisely what he said. It's a good habit, if you're dealing with Curly.

A few venturesome souls eased up through the gunsmoke hanging in the cool night air.

Curly said, "One of you go get the marshal. These two gunmen has tried to rob and kill us. And get a doctor. They's hurt bad."

Actually, they was both dead as stones.

When the doctor showed up shortly afterward, he backed up my diagnosis.

"Yep," he said, "Dead as two churchyard bricks," and then he staggered away. Back to a saloon, I guess.

Not long after that the no-account marshal got there too. "Durn," he spluttered. "Those is my last two deputies."

"Should of worn badges," Curly said. "They come at us out of a durn alley, guns drawn and saying they was gonna take our'n. Said they was working for you, but I didn't put no stock in that, since you knowed good and well we was officers of the law, on official business. They decided to use force, and when they started shooting we had to put 'em down. You didn't send them after us, now did you?"

He stuttered some more. "Naw, I never . . . that would be . . ."

Curly said, "Something like that, I'd take it as a shakedown. As personal as it gets."

"No, see, what it was, was I heard there was some heavy-armed strangers on the street, and I tole them two to bring 'em in. Had no idea it was you. Stupid boogers had silver badges I gave 'em. Probably sold 'em for drinks. Stupid boogers." Sweat was pouring down his face, and it was right cool out.

"Should of worn them durn badges," Curly said again. "Could of headed off all this sadness. I mean, how was we to know?"

★ ★ ★ ★ ★

Come morning, we settled up at the livery and lit out early for Sweetwater.

"We'll take breakfast along the trail home," Curly said, "Before that butt-hole finds hisself some more deputies. Here you go, Deputy Dent, have a new badge." He tossed me one and pinned the other on his vest. I had to catch mine up against my chest.

"Heavy silver," Curly said. "Lots nicer than the old ones we had, and always good for a drink in time of need."

It added to my feelings of flushness. On top of the gun money, we'd got another sixty for the three captured mounts.

I said, "I can get the old one off, but I might need you to help me pin on this new one. I mean, before we do any more official law stuff."

He looked at me funny.

I said, "You're looking at me funny. You mean these new ones ain't no good for official stuff? If we got to wear the old ones, why'd you . . . ?"

"Brodie, we ain't been official since we left Sweetwater. Wake up, boy. I told you they didn't want to pay for no more tracking."

"Yeah, Marshal, you said they didn't 'want' to. You didn't tell me they wasn't going to. We ain't getting paid?"

"Heck, we done just made more selling bandit goods than on any durn payroll."

I said, "Hold on, though. These killings we done on this ride. They were unofficial?"

"Not as far as they know."

I dropped both badges in my saddlebag.

CHAPTER TWENTY-NINE

Instead of following the Wichita River, we set out northwest and hit the Red River long before dark, then swung west. With the pressure off to catch Preacher and maybe some slack time ahead, my thoughts went straight to Emmalee. She'd be having that baby by spring. Maybe Byden wouldn't be a good daddy. Maybe . . .

"You thinking about those last two we killed, Brodie?"

"Uh, not exactly. How come?"

"You think I was too hard on 'em? Didn't give 'em no real chance?"

"Hell, Curly, too hard on 'em? You shot 'em. I did too, but I's following your lead. Like always."

"Here's the thing, Brodie. That was a shakedown. Had them two got us on some back street, they'da cut us down and swore it was self defense. They was studying us in that café before we ever seen the marshal. Probably already knew we was selling them horses."

I said, "So, they run and told the marshal. We said something to him about selling guns too, so you figure he had us pegged as fat targets."

"That's it. Near got us killed. Thing to remember here is, always pay attention. And don't talk too much. You got to learn something from every case, Deputy."

"I do appreciate these lessons, Marshal. I ain't sure when I talked too much, but the main thing I learned here was don't never try to shake down Curly Jack Sentell."

He snorted, and we rode on.

It was a right peaceful trip home. No sandstorm, and no rogue lawmen, aside from us. No gunfights and no rustlers, leastways no live ones. We did pass those four that Lew Turner hung. They was still swinging in the breeze, with maybe a dozen vultures tending to them. I had to look away and pull my scarf over my nose.

"Don't look away, Brodie. Let that sight burn into your brain. It'll steady you in hard times, help you remember it's important to choose your work careful."

I stared at him a minute to see if he was joking. After a bit I said, "Has it slipped your mind that this work we've chose has got us both shot up pretty good?"

"See, all you think of is the bad parts. I'd say think how Byden was there to stop your bleeding and do the cutting. Billy was there to fix you up that claw. Y'all was there to look out for me when I was shot. We was there for Billy and them women. Don't tell me we ain't lucky."

You know how you argue with that kind of reason? You don't.

He said, "You need to quit bellyaching for a while and help me watch for LT ranch line riders. Don't want them to spot us first and figger us for more bandits. We're on their range now. Did you notice every durn one of them LT boys had Remington carbines?"

I said, "If you wasn't so busy pointing up all my good fortune, you might of noticed two of them LT cowpokes is coming at us from the south. Right now. Probably got Remington carbines."

Could be Lew Turner was a butt-head and a hard man, but he sure ran a clean ranch, and his foreman Hernando made sure we ate good. Beef, beans, stewed tomatoes, pan-fried potatoes, biscuits, and milk. Lord.

Hernando said, "Sorry you miss Señor Turner, Marshal. He say his head, it hurts too much. He don't leave the hacienda now, two days."

Curly said, "He really sick or kind of hung over?"

Hernando said, "Maybe both, but sick for sure."

I said, "What happens if he dies?"

"I dunno," Hernando said. "No *muchachos*. The Señora, she's no sick, but she can't run things. And she don't trust me none."

Curly said, "Why not? Heck, you're the Number Two."

The foreman shook his head. "I think it's Señor Turner's fault. He tole her I'm a thieving Mexican, but he needs me because I'm big. And half the vaqueros are Texians, like me. We ain't no Mexicans. Hell, we ain't none of us ever even been to Mexico. I don't know, Marshal. It's dark times. I hope he don't die."

"Y'all got a doctor?"

Hernando shrugged. "He don't trust them too."

Curly said, "You probably know I don't care for the man, Se-gundo. Used to work for him myself. Still, you want me to go take a look, I'll do it. We ain't in no hurry, and I could put in a good word for you."

"For me, Marshal? *Por que?*"

"With the Señora."

"Ah. *Si. Gracias.* Squeak, take the lawmen to the hacienda. Tell the Señora the marshal is old *amigo* of the *Jefe. Muy impor-tanto.*"

It was a short ride to the main house. On the way, Squeak said, "Durn, Marshal, you got here pretty pronto after the old man got sick. You trying to cut me out of my chance at the next rich widder?"

Curly laughed. "I ain't met the lady, Squeak, but I'd guess she's a mite too old for you. Heck, she's probably too old even for an old fart like me."

She wasn't.

I mean, she was old, like Curly. Maybe thirty-five, maybe older, but she surely looked fine to me. Nice dressed, kind of small, not all heavy like most rich women was. So I heard, I mean. I don't think I ever seen a rich woman before her, but Mrs. Turner come to that door and about froze us with a warm smile. I mean, I can't speak for Curly, but I got goosebumps.

Her eyes were gun-metal gray, but sad. She just seemed nice. Next thing I knew, Curly took his hat off and was inside, me and Squeak was sitting in some rocking chairs on the porch, and a Mex girl brung us glasses of sweet lemon water.

"That her daughter, Squeak?"

"Naw, Brodie, she ain't got no kids. That there is her cook's *muchacha*. Her daddy's the blacksmith. You catch that smile she gave me?"

"In fact I did."

"We get along pretty good. She ain't a bad catch herself, but she ain't nothing like Miz Turner. You ever seen the likes of her?" He motioned like he was fanning himself.

"Nosir, in fact I have not. My take on her? Ain't none of us got as much chance with her as a Chinaman has of getting to Heaven."

Squeak sagged. "I know. Hard not to dream, though. You know what I mean?"

"In fact I do. I'm all caught up on a married lady myself, with no hope at all. Husband's a butt-head and lots older, but he ain't near death or nothing. And he's got her pregnant."

"Man," Squeak said, "You're worse off than me." He broke into a big grin. "That makes me feel some better."

Directly that Mex girl eased back out on the porch to talk to Squeak, so I excused myself to find the privy.

★ ★ ★ ★ ★

It took a while to rebutton my trousers, and when I got back around front the girl was gone and Squeak was on the steps. Curly was on the porch, hat in hand, talking to that woman.

"Miz Turner," he said, "I hate your husband ain't doing better, but I trust he'll improve. Remember what I said, now. You got a good foreman in Hernando. You can trust him with your life and ranch. The men will do what he tells 'em."

She touched his arm, and I saw her eyes had turned happy. She said, "Oh, Marshal Sentell, I can't tell you how much your visit means to me. Us. I know my husband might have seemed somewhat gruff and unresponsive, but I also know you have reassured him. Both of us."

Curly blushed. I swear. I seen it.

"It wont nothing," he muttered.

"It certainly was, too. And I feel so much better about Hernando. He's always been perfectly polite and attentive to my wishes, but for some reason my husband doesn't fully trust him."

"Could be Lew don't trust no Mex's. Or Texians. They's a good measure of men like that. More likely is he don't trust no men when it comes to you. Now as I've met you, I can see why."

Now she blushed. What little I'd seen of Lew Turner, I guess she didn't get too many compliments from that corner.

"Why, Marshal . . ." she stammered.

"No, it's true. Now I got to ride, before I step on my own durn tongue. But I'm only up to Sweetwater. Maybe a hundred miles. You need help, tell Hernando to send for me."

"Thank you, Marshal. I would feel comfortable doing that."

It was kind of a quiet ride north. I mean, as quiet as it could be, what with the wind gusting and the horses clopping along and blowing every now and then, clacking their bits, leather squeaking and all. Wasn't no talking.

Finally, Curly turned in his saddle and looked back. He said, "Was she something, or what?"

I don't think he was talking to me, but I knew exactly what he meant. I felt the same about Emmalee.

CHAPTER THIRTY

We crested a rise midmorning and there was Sweetwater before us, right where it had always been. Maybe.

Problem was the sign on the main road south said, "Welcome to Mobeetie, Texas." It had a population number that had been changed twice and sported a few bullet holes, but it surely said, "Mobeetie."

Curly gave me a funny look, pulled off his hat, and scratched his bald top. "Ain't that the Rath and Hanrahan store, right there?"

I said, "It truly is. And over there's the Alley Cat Saloon. And the Lady Gay. And there's Godiva Jones, coming outta the store." Wasn't nobody else moving so early.

He yelled, "Godiva!"

She pranced right over, holding her hat against the wind, and give us her best smile. "Marshal, Brodie. Welcome back. Good ride?"

"Never mind that, girl. What is this 'Mobeetie' business? We get taken over by durn Comanches or something?"

"Nossir, Marshal. Whyn't y'all buy me some ham and eggs and I'll 'splain it to you, best I can."

Over food and coffee, she said, "Town leaders went and asked for a post office, but the state folks said 'Sweetwater' was already took. Down south, west of Abilene. A whole 'nuther town right alongside a whole 'nuther Sweetwater Creek. Don't that beat all?"

"Truly," said Curly. "But where'd they come up with this new name?"

"They asked some old Injin what the Injin word was for 'Sweetwater' and he tole 'em it was 'Mobeetie.' So now we got a Injin name and a post office." She pulled a flask from her purse and poured a little whiskey in her coffee. "We get us a rail line in here, we'll be doing our business in high cotton."

Curly said, "For a second or two there, me and Brodie thought we'd done zigged when we shoulda zagged and come up in the wrong place. Is 'Mobeetie' Comanch or Kioway talk?"

Godiva said, "Who knows? Could be Tonk. Who cares? It's Injin, Curly. You gonna have to learn to live with it."

He muttered, "Well, it could mean different things to different Injins. For all we know, it could mean sheep piss."

Turns out that was one translation, though we didn't learn that fact for some time. Might be why the railway never came through.

Anyways, I guess there's some old Indian still laughing about his trick. Could be entire tribes that joke about it.

Town leaders was happy to see us back, as they was unhappy about folks shooting up their signs. They wouldn't pay us for our Wichita Falls trip, but they put us back on the payroll straight away.

First order of business was stopping the loose use of gunfire in our little town.

"What do we do, Marshal? Shoot a few, get their attention?"

"Naw, Brodie. Mainly they's drunk boys who ain't been paid no attention, coming off a cattle drive or a resupply wagon train from Fort Dodge and needing to sleep it off."

"You might get to show me right soon. Take a gander at that fat freighter at the card table behind you."

Curly turned sideways to look at the brewing problem, right

as the fat man slammed his cards down and said, "Something ain't right."

The man knocked his stool over as he got up, then stepped away, turned in a circle, and stood splay-legged. He stuck his chin out and huffed some. "Ain't no way you could win so much. Average laws, or something like that."

Curly was suddenly between him and the gamblers at the table. He said, "Could be that you're too drunk to win. Sleep it off and try it sober." He said it easy, and he was smiling.

The big man said, "Stay outta this, old man."

He should have noticed Curly's badge and the fact that Curly's right hand was resting on the butt of a Schofield revolver, which about then flashed out of that cross-draw rig and clipped him beside his right eye. He went down.

Curly looked over at me. "See? Now he can sleep it off. Would a couple of you folks help me get him to the jail? I ain't sure y'all were fleecing him, but it looked to be a near thing."

All four gamblers jumped up and tried to lift him, but he was at least two hundred fifty pounds of dead weight.

Curly waved that pistol generally at the barkeep who was suddenly eager to help too.

"Jasper," Curly said, "Lift that backroom door off'n its hinges and help put this boy on it. I'll send it back once we got him locked away."

"Yessir. Yessir, Mister Marshal. Happy to oblige. I was fixing to cut him off."

Curly nailed him with that stare. I had to learn that. He said, "Well, Jasper, I'd say you was a shade slow. Good thing I was here to head off a shoot-out. Stuff mighta got broke, people hurt. You, maybe. Bad for business."

As they dumped the freighter on a jail cot, Curly said to me, "Problem with good old boys like him? They get drunk and lucky, they can kill you. You can't talk 'em out of nothing. Only reason I speak to 'em before I whack 'em is to put 'em off guard. I'm still gonna whack 'em."

I said, "Every time?"

He said, "Less'n I shoot 'em. You notice I wear my Schofield in town?"

"Yes I did."

He said, "It's a measure better for whacking."

Back on the street, I said, "Now, if they cleaned him out, who'll stand for his fine?"

Curly said, "It's only five dollars. Them gamblers and the bartender will cover it. Only a dollar each."

"You know this, for a fact?"

He laughed. "I do, Brodie. I'll invite 'em to. Ain't likely they'll displease me."

We headed for the Lady Gay, starting our rounds of the saloons.

"You say you whack 'em or shoot 'em, Marshal. What if that man had turned and walked away?"

He said, "Happened to me once, back when I started lawing. Feller walked off five steps, spun back, and pulled on me. Fired, too, but missed."

"You kill him?"

"Not right off. Took him two days to die. Since then, if they turn away they gonna get whacked on the back of the head. You let 'em get out of reach, you probably gonna have to shoot 'em. They's better off if you go ahead and whack 'em."

I said, "I heard some call it buffaloing."

He said, "I heard that too, but to my mind, buffaloing somebody means fooling 'em."

About that time, a young cowpoke came reeling out of the Lady Gay Saloon. He caught his balance, spotted us, and shouted, "Hey! Lawmen. Y'all come here."

I noticed he was wearing an old cap and ball Navy Colt. Hair on my neck stood right out.

Curly, on the other hand, smiled at him and walked right up to him. I followed, but I was wired tight.

Curly said, "Yessir?"

The boy, who might have been eighteen, said, "Whore in there? Redhead? She says she won't give me no poke. I got money and I know my rights. You go in there and straighten her out before I take the law in my own hands . . ."

Curly said, "Deputy, show him your claw."

I held it up and when the boy tried to focus on it, Curly whacked him.

"Now him, you see, ain't no worry about no fine. He done tole us he's got plenty of money. You starting to get this?"

I said, "I am. But I got to tell you that it'd be legal to say you buffaloed that boy."

Things started to get more quiet that very day.

Curly said, "How long we been back here now, two months?"

We were drinking coffee in the Alley Cat. I said, "Something like that. Why?"

"Seems it's got too quiet hereabouts," he said. "Town council figgers we don't need no full-time deputy. You got some place you'd care to visit?"

"In fact I do."

He grinned. "I figgered as much. I'll get your pay."

CHAPTER THIRTY-ONE

It was a bitter cold ride to Tascosa. Wind, of course, but spitting snow too. Enough to color the ground but not so much as to drift. I had a glove on my gun hand and wore my heaviest coat, which wont all that heavy.

I went straight to the blacksmith's. It's one place you can count on having a fire, and Billy was one reason I was there.

Billy and Conchita danced around me like the children they were. After my teeth quit chattering, we got caught up some on one another.

The blacksmith and Señora Terrazas joined in. He remembered me, but I guess it's not easy to forget somebody with a steel claw.

"You saved my woman and our baby girl and brought 'em home. My name's Kendall."

I shook hands and said, "Yessir, but ain't her name Miz Terrazas? How come it ain't Kendall too?"

"Yep," he said. "We ain't true married. Her man Terrazas got hisself killed years back so she took up with me when I got here. And I took Conchita as my own. And now we got Billy."

"How's he doing?" I asked.

"Smart as a durn whip. 'Course, you know that. How's that claw?"

I said, "Lemme show you." I drew my belt pistol and used the claw to eject a round, then picked up my carbine and jacked the lever to throw out a cartridge from it too.

To top it off, I bent and picked up each shell from the floor using my claw and thumb, and dropped them on the table before reloading them.

He smiled and said, "Now, that's all right. Billy, you done good work there, son." He pointed at my claw and did a thumbs-up. He used a lot of little signs, for Conchita I guess.

Billy and Conchita was grinning ear to ear.

"Something I might could do for you, though," Kendall continued. "Billy, toss him your Colt."

I caught it and said, "This ain't the one I gave you."

Billy was nodding and smiling. "Is too," he said.

Kendall said, "That seven-and-a-half-inch barrel was a shade too long for him on the draw. I cut it back to five inches, remounted the sight."

"Durn," I said. "It feels good." I handed it back.

"Tell him," Billy said.

"All right, son, I'll tell him. See, Brodie, couple weeks back this young cowpuncher had him a few shots of bust-head and tried to get sideways with Conchita. When Billy told him to ease off, he went for his pistol. Billy pulled and covered him in a wink. Scared the piss out of that boy."

I said, "Looks like it ended all right. Did Billy whack him?"

"No. Didn't have to. He had Conchita take the boy's pistol and empty it, then give it back and told him to ride."

"You did that, Billy?" I was right astounded.

Billy nodded, and the blacksmith said, "Next thing I knowed, here come the foreman from that cow camp telling me he didn't want none of his boys shot up by no mankiller, even if they's in the likker and might deserve it. Wanted to know could we work out something less permanent than killing."

I was laughing too hard to comment.

He went on. "I tole him if they'd leave the women and children and sheep and sheepherders alone, I'd ask our mankiller to cut 'em some slack. Anyways, I could take some off the front end of your belt gun too. Take off the ejector too, cut it down to maybe four inches, do you want it really light and fast."

I handed it right over. "Now, what about Emmalee Byden," I said.

Billy and Conchita both signalled she was showing.

Kendall said, "I'd say she's healthy. I don't know as I'd say she's happy."

I said, "What do you mean?"

"I mean, if I treated Miz Terrazas same as Byden does that nice young wife of his, Miz Terrazas would run my ass off or beat me to death with a fry pan. Now, you ain't tole me what length you want on this barrel."

"Cut it all you can and still leave the ejector."

They steered me toward the Byden cabin. Rawley Byden must of been off doing whatever sheepherders do during the day. Counting sheep, maybe, or chasing off wolves. With me around, that wont too bad a skill to have.

She said, "In the kitchen" when I knocked, and that's where I found her. She didn't look up right away.

She said, "Thanks for coming, Señora Terrazas. I'm not sure how long to cook that . . . Oh, my God, Brodie!"

She dropped a pan of biscuits on the floor and ran to hug me, getting us both covered with flour.

I stood there sort of struck dumb, barely patting her back. Scared to really hug her in return, as I was no way sure how that might play out, and her mumbling and snuffling the whole time, stuff like, "too long," "worried," and "missing."

She pushed back pretty quick and knuckled her eyes and muttered, "So silly," then said, "I was expecting the Señora, but . . . Brodie, do you know much about cooking a leg of lamb?"

She pointed to this big hunk of meat and bone in a pan, and then we both broke out laughing so hard it's a wonder we didn't both bust a gut.

After we got down to where we were only giggling and spitting, I said, "I don't know squat about cooking, but I could give you a hand."

She snorted and said, "Another one?" and that set us off again.

I can tell you that up to right then, that was the happiest three or four minutes of my life. I didn't know I could laugh like that.

The laughter passed and we were quiet for a minute or two, just looking at each other. I couldn't help glancing at her stomach.

"Huge, isn't it?" she said, patting it. "You want to feel it?"

"I better not."

"Brodie, I'm sorry I joked about you losing your hand over me. I'm so comfortable with you, and I feel like you know I would never say anything to hurt you."

"It didn't hurt, Emmalee. Heck, I thought it was funny as all get-out."

"May I look at it, Brodie? To see how it healed?"

I undid the thong that held the can and claw and slid it off my forearm. She peeled off some cloth ticking I put over the end every morning.

"It looks like it's healed nicely, Brodie. I see you keep it clean. Does it itch or hurt at all?"

"Doesn't hurt a bit, Emmalee. Only itches if somebody asks about it."

I scratched it and she laughed again, but then she took it in both hands and kissed the nub and thumb. She held it against her cheek and looked straight at me, and durn if tears didn't pop out on her face.

"For me," she said. "I mean, me and the other women."

I couldn't talk. There was so many feelings boiling up in me right then that I couldn't name them nor explain them.

And, of course, that's when her husband walked in.

Chapter Thirty-Two

Rawley Byden shucked his hat, gloves, and coat, but his eyes kept flicking from her to me. She let go of my arm and dropped her hands into her lap.

"Wondered whose horse that was. Should of known, I guess." His voice started normal, but got louder as he talked. "Now, what the hell is going on here? In my home, in broad daylight?"

"Not a thing, Rawley," she said, as calm as you please. "It's only two good friends talking is all."

He was hot, and getting hotter. I went to rest my hand on my gun butt, out of habit for tense times, but it was in the blacksmith's shop.

He fairly yelled, "And you talking is how you got flour dust all over you both? And why's the claw off, Dent? Didn't want to tear her dress? Is that it?"

"You got no call to say no such thing," I said. "Ain't neither one of us ever done a thing wrong or to shame you."

"Really?" he roared. "You ain't supposed to be alone with my wife. Not anywhere, but 'specially not in my home."

"Byden, slow down. I didn't know you wasn't here when I came over, and she didn't know it was me when she yelled to come in. I startled her is all, and that's how come the flour got spilled."

"Who'd you think he was, Emmalee? The durn President, maybe?"

"Señora Terrazas was going to come help me with cooking

150

that leg of lamb, Rawley. I thought it was her. There's nothing here. Maybe, if you will stop looking for something that doesn't exist, you won't make a total fool of yourself."

He snorted. "The whole thing is a likely story."

"It is," she said, as she slid that can back over my wrist and retied the thong. "But it isn't totally accurate. He did startle me, but the reason we have flour all over us is that I hugged him, because I was so happy to see him again. All right? And I think you've forgotten what he gave up for us."

He stood there with his mouth working and nothing coming out, blinking like crazy.

She turned to me. "As I said, it's healing well, and we can never make up for your loss, but I want to see you whenever you come to visit Billy. And I apologize for my husband's total rudeness."

I nodded and headed for the door. I thought it was over, but he all of a sudden grabbed a poker from the fireplace and said, "I ought to . . ."

I didn't have a gun, but I do wear a heavy Bowie with a ten-inch blade. I pulled it, and put my claw arm up to block his swing. He stopped.

"I'm leaving, but you come at me with that hot iron, I'm gonna do my best to cut off your durn hand."

He backed up and tossed the poker in the fire, sending out a shower of sparks. "Get out of my house. And stay out."

I said, "I said I's leaving. But don't you push me none. Not ever. Emmalee, I'm sorry to cause such a fuss. He is a rude man, but I knew that and I shoulda stayed away."

I opened the door to a blast of cold wind, but turned back for a parting shot. I spoke to her, but stared at him. "He ever hurts you and I hear tell, I'll most likely come kill him."

I slammed the door, mounted, and rode back to the blacksmith's place to spend the night. Couldn't help thinking I was glad Byden didn't start in on me with that hot poker. I don't know how that would of turned out. I decided I need to keep a gun on my person at all times.

All right, maybe not all times. Bathing, for example, and other stuff not involving too many clothes. But nearby, no matter what.

I had no real reason to hang around Tascosa after that, but I had nowhere to go and no possibility of leaving, not right off. The snow got serious that same evening and we were penned up good for several days.

Before you could whistle Dixie I had a bad case of cabin fever added to my "No-Emmalee-Itis." Soon as the weather broke a little I decided to make a wide swing to the south, visit some of the cattle ranches that was popping up, and see if anybody had seen or heard of Preacher Vance and his gang. Besides, my cut-down Colt was ready to be tried out.

Billy decided to go with me. Maybe fourteen now, and he decided. Didn't ask me or nothing.

"Getting right growed up, ain't you?" I said as we crossed the river.

"Some," he answered, then pointed. "Boggy creek," he said.

We swung left some, to cross east of the bog. Ten miles south we started bumping into cattle, some of them dead. They'd push up against any kind of wind break and the snow would drift up and kill them. "Coyotes and wolves is gonna have a fine time once this melts some," I said.

Billy pointed to some riders heading our way. We drew our carbines, but they was only cowpokes watching for rustlers. I showed them my pretty silver badge, and we traded talk and rode on to do it again and again.

Twenty miles south and hadn't nobody seen nor heard of the preacher. We stopped and shared a fire and some beans with two young line riders.

And steak. They'd just cut up a froze cow. One of them said, "So, what is you the marshal of?"

I started to tell him noplace, that I used to be a deputy, and that the badge headed off bad thoughts, for the most part.

Before I could speak, Billy said, "Tascosa."

That was a lot better answer than I come up with.

One of the boys said, "Jumping Jehosophat. That's a tough little town. And with a claw."

The other one cut me another slab of beef. I decided to let that little fib ride.

"My deputy there is the fast one," I said.

Billy didn't even look up. He nodded and kept eating. Heck, he was near as old as them, and acted older. Seen more, I guess.

We cut west the next morning, and the next two days was more of the same. No sign of Preacher Vance.

Still and all, I don't figure that ride was wasted. Word got out to the cow camps that there was law in Tascosa.

Couldn't hurt none. Durn sure wasn't no good like it was, and we never said we was elected.

CHAPTER THIRTY-THREE

Four days of riding in that cold and I was ready to suffer some more cabin fever. We crossed the Canadian back to the north side and I felt like I was coming home.

Señora Terrazas loaded us up on baked mutton and fried lamb, which was my favorite. I kept watching for some sign of Emmalee, but only seen her once, on her way to the privy. Of course I couldn't speak then.

After two days, I grabbed Billy and said, "You go over there and tell her and Byden what we did, and that there's no sign of Preacher yet."

He said, "Me tell?" He laughed and turned to the Señora and spoke some Mex with her. I swear he talked better Mex than English.

She wrapped up and hustled out and was back in no time, looking worried.

I said, "What's wrong?"

She wouldn't look at me, but started yapping at Kendall. He could really talk Mex.

He turned to me and said, "She says Miz Byden wants to know when you're leaving."

"Soon as the snow melts some more, I guess. What's wrong? I can see something's wrong."

Kendall said, "No concern of yours. Looks like Miz Byden is putting something together for you to take to Mobeetie. Be ready in a day or so. Wanted you to wait, if you can."

I said, "Well, I guess I can."

My heart about jumped out of my chest.

Billy went to tell her.

The next two days flowed by about as fast as molasses on a cold day. I fretted, I cleaned my guns, I helped old Kendall make some horseshoes and put them on a horse, I oiled my claw, I fretted some more. None of it necessary, and none of it helped.

Third morning, Kendall went out for a few minutes, then come back and said something to Billy. Billy nodded and took off in a hurry, pulling on his coat as he run out the door.

"What's going on?" I said.

The blacksmith said, "I seen Byden ride north just now, so I sent Billy to see is your, uh, this thing is ready."

I said, "I could of gone."

He said, "Brodie, that ain't a good idea."

Not ten minutes passed before Billy was back, toting a sheepskin coat. For me. Made by Emmalee Byden.

Everyone has seen them. Skin on the outside, wool inside and around the collar. Oversized sleeves to allow for a jacket and my claw. Not so long as my slicker, and plenty of room for my gunbelt under it when it was closed up. Rope loops on the front to hook over wood buttons. Heck, even I could handle them.

"This is the nicest thing I ever got," I said.

Everybody in the Kendall household agreed.

"I got to go and show her. And thank her."

Everybody shook their heads to say no.

I packed up and was ready to ride in an hour. They all came out to wave goodbye and wish me luck.

I made it all the way to the river before I turned back and rode straight to Emmalee's front door. I banged on the door several times and said, "I know you're in there."

A few minutes went by, but then she said, "I knew you'd come. I knew it, but you can't come in. You have to ride on, Brodie, and leave me be. It's what's best for me."

Well, that stopped me. I didn't want to cause her no more pain than I might have already.

"I sure like my coat," I said. "It fits real good, and it's warm as can be. I ain't ever had anything so nice."

"I'm happy for that, Brodie. Truly I am. Now you have to leave before he comes back."

I headed for Mobeetie, every bit as sad as I'd been happy a few days before.

I don't even know for sure why I rode back to Mobeetie. I didn't have a job there, it's a hundred durn miles from Tascosa and Emmalee Byden, and it was a long cold ride, even with my new coat.

Curly said as much when I walked in his office.

"I don't see why you come back, Brodie. I can't pay you, and you ain't got nobody here. Seems to me you near froze your nuts off for nothing."

I said, "Well, there's Godiva Jones."

"I was about to talk to you about that," he said. "She's took up with another freighter."

"So?"

"This one owns three wagons. And he ain't fat."

"Durn," I said. "That ain't good. I guess it's back to Saw-Tooth Sally."

"She's with me."

"Curly," I said, "I can't stand no more of your good cheer. I'll be drinking in the Lady Gay, if it ain't burned down or been carried off by Comanche raiders."

★　★　★　★　★

That's sort of how that winter passed, easing on into 1880. There was hundreds of rough characters who'd come to town to sit out the worst weather, and white sergeants and officers would come in from Fort Elliott. Buffalo soldiers had their own place, the Ring Town Saloon, out near the fort. That held down some trouble, as there was a measure of folks who still didn't cater to darkies.

Still, Mobeetie was a wild and dangerous place. Main reasons I survived was I didn't have enough money to drink myself to death, and the fact that Curly Sentell tole everybody that I was a short-fused mankiller, crazy over the loss of my hand and a woman. He was pretty near right.

Curly gave me as much part-time deputy work as he could, but my money supply eventually gave out. I had just spent my last two bits on breakfast, and here come Godiva Jones' big freighter.

I figured he found out I was spending time with her whenever he left on a run. When it rains, it floods. I put my hand on my gun butt.

"Mister Dent?"

Mister Dent? I thought, what on earth is this, and where is it going?

"Yessir?" I said.

"I'm C.W. Knowlton. Folks call me Punch."

I said, "I know you, Knowlton."

"All right. That's good. I guess you know I got two wagons? Make runs to Fort Supply and Dodge City, mostly."

I said, "Thought you had three."

"I did, Mister Dent, but one was took, last trip. It's what I want to ask you about."

"Well, I durn sure didn't take it. I ain't left town in a month. Ain't hardly left this saloon."

157

"Yessir, Mister Dent, I know that. I wasn't insinuating nothing. It was a jackleg gang of breeds, out east of the old Springer Trading Post. I'm hoping I can hire you to ride guard for me. Twenny dollars a trip."

I was saved. I stood up. "Are you serious?"

He mistook my little outburst.

"All right, all right. Twenny-five. I can't lose no more wagons."

I nearly choked. "All right. I can do that, but I ain't riding on no wagon."

"Nossir. You can ride anyways you want. I am right pleased, Mister Dent, right pleased indeed."

He was right excited and jumpy is what he was. He reached to shake my hand but I was still too nervous to let go of my Colt. I gave him my claw, and he jumped a little when it kind of punctured his palm.

"That's all right. It's fine. My fault. Can you go today? Maybe this morning?"

I said, "I can, but I need an advance to settle up at the livery and rent me a spare horse. I, uh, I don't want to spend my own money on your business."

"Yessir," he said, pulling a wad of bills, "Here's ten up front. Only right. And I'll provide that spare mount and tell the livery to get your horse ready. And thank you, Mister Dent."

I said, "Well, then, I'll stop by the privy, pick up my saddle guns and bedroll, and be at the livery in fifteen, twenty minutes. And call me Brodie."

I guess there's an upside to being thought of as a short-fused mankiller, who's a little crazy.

He said, "Fine . . . that's good. I'll go rush up my boys, get us ready too. I feel good about this, Mister . . . Brodie. Yessir I do."

Fifteen minutes later I was kissing Godiva Jones goodbye. I

knew where her freighter was. Heckfire, we could look out her window and see him, down by the stables.

CHAPTER THIRTY-FOUR

C. W. Knowlton had a couple of stout bull-whackers as drivers, and him and another man riding shotgun. Both drivers had ten-gauge doubles behind their seats. Everybody had at least one revolver.

And then there was me. Two Colts across my pommel, both forty-four-forties, like my belt gun and my carbine. Loaded for bear. I remember thinking, if I was leading a jackleg gang of breeds, I wouldn't try us out. I was wrong.

We crossed the Canadian River at the stage station and angled northeast to hit Wolf Creek.

I said, "I'd be surprised if those boys bother us this trip, heavy armed as we are. How far to Camp Supply?"

Knowlton said, "It's called Fort Supply now. We're maybe halfway now from Canadian Station. And I think you're right, Brodie. They'll want to catch us on the way back, loaded with likker and dry goods."

He was wrong too. He hadn't no more than spoke when I spotted movement, a half mile ahead. I got my glass on them, straight away.

Knowlton said, "What is it?"

I said, "Looks like maybe we was doing some wishful think-ing. Now, y'all don't make any sudden moves, but get those shotguns up beside you. They's maybe six of 'em by that stand of trees on that ridge over to the right a little. Now four has peeled away back over the ridge. Other two are riding to cut us off."

Knowlton said, "This might be the same ones. What do we do? Circle and fight?"

I said, "Keep on our path. Let me talk. If I start shooting, feel free to join in. For all I know, this could be a posse looking for them same bandits we's worried about."

One of the drivers said, "I thought you wasn't worried."

"I wasn't. Now I am." I unshucked my carbine.

They weren't no posse. One of the men riding up to us was none other than "Black Turkey" Creek Jackson. I didn't know his partner, but I'd arrested Jackson for horse stealing back when I was a Ranger. A so-called jury let him off.

As the bandits got close I told Knowlton's men, "Y'all hold right here, and keep a sharp lookout for them others." I dismounted and tied off to a bush. Didn't want to be on no bucking horse if the dance started here. Drew my carbine, checked the chamber, and cocked it.

Creek Jackson and his partner pulled up maybe twenty steps away.

I said, "Well, Turkey, I'm surprised to see you alive. And not in jail."

He was a little older than me. Half Creek, half darky. Mean as a snake. Liked to cut folks.

He said, "Well, if it ain't the young Ranger. I heard you ain't Rangering no more. And you're starting to lose parts."

I said, "State your business, Turkey."

"My name ain't Turkey, and you know it. You call me Black Turkey, or you call me Creek. You can even say Turkey Creek, but not Turkey, you hear?"

"That your business? Telling folks what to call you?"

I think he bit his tongue. He said, "My business, lawdog, is protecting people. You pay us a little, we make sure you get to

Fort Supply. Even Dodge."

I said, "Now, here's the thing. I ain't the law, so I can't arrest you for no shakedown. But you are a turkey. Will be 'til you die."

I'm not sure he went for his gun. It don't matter. He was too far away to whack, so I shot him. That Winchester slug knocked him right out of the saddle.

C. W. Knowlton froze, but the other shotgun guard tried to kill Turkey's partner. He missed with one barrel but his second shot hit the man in the leg pretty good and killed his horse.

"Hold fire!" I yelled. "Keep watch, like I said. Knowlton, pull that boy out from under his horse and get his guns. One of you bring Turkey's horse here. Toss his carbine in your wagon."

I eased over to Turkey. He wasn't doing too good. Blood was bubbling up from his chest and he was kind of coughing and spitting it too. I shot him in the head. He went stiff-legged for a instant, then lay still.

I walked over to the other one. He was having trouble standing.

"You gonna kill me too?" he whispered. Probably in some pain. He looked to be half Mex and half Indian.

"Maybe," I said. "Maybe not today. You get on his horse, go tell your gang what happened here. Tell 'em to get a good look at these wagons and stay shed of 'em."

"*Si, Señor. Bueno.*"

"Another thing, Bueno. Is any of them others you with called Preacher?"

"No, *Señor. Muchachos*, is all. The Padre? He is in Mexico, so I hear. Now, can I take my saddle? It's a very nice saddle. Not a old piece of shit like Black Turkey rode."

The boy had some *cojones*. I said, "It is a nice saddle. I mean to sell it in Fort Supply. You can go there and buy it back, long as we don't cross paths. Next time I see you, I mean to kill you."

He shrugged, mounted, and rode east.

He was right about that saddle. It was a fine Mexican-made Pueblo saddle, fancy as could be. Nickel horn, which wasn't no good for roping but durn sure looked nice.

I rode it the next day. It was well broke in and felt good. When we got to Fort Supply I sold my old Texas rig and kept the pretty one. Wasn't like I was going to ever do no more roping. Wasn't nothing wrong with my old rig, neither. I got forty dollars for it. Better than some horses I've sold.

The trip home was about as cold, but not so exciting. Only gunfire was Knowlton shotgunning a few grouse and me knocking down a pronghorn and a gobbler. We ate pretty good.

Third night on the way back and us settling in, Knowlton said, "You been pretty rough on turkeys this trip."

One of the drivers busted out laughing. It took me and the others a minute to catch on.

"Pretty good one, C.W." I said. I was disliking him less each day. "We get home, old Curly is likely to start calling me a half-crazy birdkiller."

When he stopped laughing, C.W. said, "I want to ask you something, Brodie."

"All right."

"Folks has told me that Godiva used to be your woman, long afore I got here. I hope there ain't no hard feelings there. I mean, you don't act like there is. I was worried about asking you for help, but Godiva said you wouldn't mind."

"No hard feeling at all, C.W. She's better off with you and it's her choice, anyways. I've always liked her, but she's always looked out for herself. If she thought I was the better catch, she'd drop your butt like a hot potato. And it ain't like you've took her off the market."

He took a deep breath and nodded. "Thing is, Brodie, I really like her. I'd take her off the market tomorrow, but I don't know how it would set with her."

"She'll say yes or she'll say no. She don't beat around the bush."

"Yeah, Brodie, but if we get hitched, is she gonna still be selling pokes every time I leave town?"

"You asking me about women? Ain't you noticed I don't have one? Heckfire, C.W., I'm hung up on a durn married woman that's having a baby. And won't have nothing to do with me. Am I in a fix, or what?"

"I'm sorry. I just, well, I just figgered you knew Godiva better'n most people."

"Well, to answer you, C.W., I'd say as long as you don't let her go hungry, don't go hitting her and such, she'll probably hang on to you like a rat terrier."

"You think, Brodie? You really think?"

"Lord, C.W., it ain't a easy life she leads. And she has a good heart. You know that much, surely."

"I do." He sat there staring in the fire awhile. "I guess I'll have to fight a lot, if I go through with this. Men getting smart-mouthed, and all."

I said, "Only if she's worth it. And you won't be fighting nobody worth a hoot themselves. Me or Curly gets to 'em first, you won't be fighting 'em at all. Get some sleep."

"I believe I will. I believe I'll sleep pretty good. And I believe I'll ask you to stand up with me, if she says yes."

"Why would you do that, C.W.?"

"You standing with me? And not laughing? Who *is* gonna laugh?"

I thought the other guard and drivers were already sleeping, but one of them said, "Damn sure won't be me."

CHAPTER THIRTY-FIVE

C.W. Knowlton was serious about hitching up with Godiva, and when it was done, wasn't hardly nobody in Mobeetie had ever seen the likes of it.

Knowlton had some money. He bought Godiva a nice dress, brought in a bunch of fancy food and liquor, rented the Alley Cat, and even talked Reverend Watty into doing the wedding. Watty was the chaplain from out to Fort Elliott.

It went well, I'd say. Nobody got shot. C.W. only had one fight, and he held his own until Curly stepped in and whacked the other man. Curly had made me temporary deputy again. Didn't have to hit nobody.

I know I had never seen anything like it. Seemed like everybody had a good time, especially Godiva and Knowlton. It left me even more down than before. I guess it showed.

Curly got onto me about it as we made our rounds. He started in slow.

"You hear about that skinny whore from the Lady Gay?"

I shook my head.

"Drank too much," he said. "Set out to go throw up. Stumbled out back, missed the privy by maybe fifty yards in broad daylight. Stepped in a durn snake den."

"Lord," I said. "She live?"

He said, "Don't hardly nobody die of a twisted ankle. It's barely Spring. Them rattlers was hardly moving. Probably scared them worse'n her."

"Curly," I said, "Why you even telling me this?"

"Saw-Tooth Sally got on me for not watching out for the whores. Said you and me near let that girl die whilst we was only watching out for rich businessmen." He stopped and spun me sideways to face him. "Brodie, do you even know any rich businessmen?"

I thought a minute. "No, Curly, I am sure I do not. C.W. thinks he's rich, but he ain't."

He started walking again. "Me, neither. I tole her you and me been taking care of whores since we was boys."

He was right. I nodded, but I still didn't know where he was heading.

"You, now, Mister Brodie Dent, you done got off the path. Fretting over a married woman, a hundred miles away, that's one thing. Here now, though, here you are moping over a whore who give up on you and nailed down some security whilst she could. You blame her? Surely not. You ain't that way."

Now, I cared a lot for Godiva Jones. All right, Godiva Knowlton. I spent nights nursing her through nightmares, I beat the snot out of a few cowpokes and gamblers that misused her. We laughed some and didn't hardly argue. We didn't expect much of each other. Heck, she knew I didn't have any substance to speak of.

Still, all that brought me to a point I didn't think I'd live to see. You know how folks say there's a first time for everything? You believe that, really? Me neither. Not 'til right then.

I was there, the first time Curly Jack Sentell was wrong. About anything.

See, I wasn't moping over Godiva. I was happy for her. I was stone-cold total messed up over Emmalee Byden. Wasn't any way he was ever going to understand, neither.

"Curly," I said, "As usual, you are as right as rain."

"I knew I was," he said. "Tell you what. With it getting a

shade warmer, you and me will ride up to Dodge and see if we can't scare up a couple of new whores. Got to replace Godiva, anyways. I bet Knowlton will let us use one of his wagons to bring 'em back."

I said, "I know for sure he will if we pay him."

Curly snorted, "Aw, we'll haul some hides up there for him. Anyways, it ought to make for a fun trip home."

It wasn't a bad trip up, either. The owner of the Lady Gay sent his madam, a healthy older woman of about thirty, to do the selecting. She took care of us and the driver all the way to Dodge.

Dodge City was always wild, and this time wasn't no different. We was eating dinner in the Long Branch when a dandy little gambler got in a dispute with a really big bull-whacker, who pulled a knife.

The dandy drew a sawed-off conversion Navy with bone grips and said, "Let's use pistols. Draw your piece and make ready."

You could see right off that the big man was having second thoughts.

"It ain't fair, y'all. I'm a bigger target than him." He looked around for support.

The dandy snapped his finger at the bartender. "Sam," he said, "Take your chalk and sketch out a man my size on him. Any of my shots that hit outside the chalk don't count."

The big man put his knife away and said, "I don't want to shoot with you. You'd likely kill me."

"Likely I would, friend. As you would likely kill me in a knife fight. You should run along now. Out you go." With a wave of his pistol, the gambler dismissed the big man, who backed out.

Most of the rest of us had ducked down behind tables and chairs as soon as they stood and faced off. As we eased back into our seats, the big man burst back in, shouting and firing a revolver.

He winged the bartender and one working girl, but not bad.

Still seated, the dandy drew and thumbed off three shots, fast. All three hit home. The big man stopped, lurched sideways over a chair, and then fell on a table, upending it. He never twitched. All three shots would of been in the chalk.

The trip back to Mobeetie was as good as Curly said it might be. The two new hires were grateful to be leaving such a hellhole as Dodge City, and Kansas in general.

See, we had told them what a paradise Mobeetie was. And the Panhandle in general.

CHAPTER THIRTY-SIX

We got back into Mobeetie late in the day. After dropping the madam and the new girls off at the Lady Gay, Curly cut Knowlton's driver loose. We still had rooms at the boardinghouse and the bath house was next door.

We took our gear up to the rooms, then paid two Chinee boys from the bath house to take our horses to the livery. Old Chin Wu ran the bath house and the laundry, so two hours later we were scrubbed and clean dressed.

Curly said, "You take the rest of the laundry by the room. I'll check at my office and meet you back at the Lady Gay for a drink and a steak before I start my rounds. See if I can get you hired back on as Deputy. Or maybe stableboy."

"I'll walk with you, whether they pay me or not. Four hundred miles in that saddle and I'm in need of a stretch," I said. "Leastways, I will be once I'm on the outside of some steak and beer."

As I crossed the street to the saloon, I had to dodge two of Knowlton's wagons hauling fresh-cut boards back toward his place from the sawmill. I thought, yep, little Miz Godiva is going to be well took care of, hooked up with a smart and busy man like Knowlton.

As I started to step inside, I heard Knowlton shouting orders behind me and turned to see the wagon we'd just let go of was being loaded with dry goods and such. Hadn't even unhitched the team yet.

I watched for a minute or two. Barrels of nails, saws, mallets, flour, beans. No way they were heading out that late, so it had to be a set-up for a early run the next day. I wondered why, but was too hungry to go ask.

I went in and ordered two steaks with beans and peppers, along with a tub of beer. The food got there before Curly, but not before Knowlton.

"Brodie," he said, pulling up a chair. "Thought I saw you come in. You've been gone a while."

"Two weeks, I'd guess," I said. "That's Curly's steak, but he ain't here yet and it's cooling. Why don't you eat it and I'll order another for him."

"Done ate, thank you. Here's the thing, Brodie. I'm glad you got back today. You seen I got me a third wagon again? Got my wagons all loaded? I mean to make a run in the morning. Be gone maybe a week, ten days."

"So, you're looking for me to ride guard again?"

"I am. Can you go again so soon?"

"That ain't a problem, C.W., but the marshal has went to see if the town would put me back on the payroll. Heck, that really ain't a problem either. You pay better, and Curly can handle this town fine by hisself."

Knowlton gave me a funny look. I hate it when that happens. He said, "I guess you ain't been back long enough to get much news."

I took another bite and said, "About all I've heard since we got in is Chinee jibber-jabber. Where you heading, that's doing so much building?"

He said, "Tascosa is growing hand over foot and they's building like crazy. I figger to get in on it. Will you go?"

"Tascosa? Let me give that some careful thought for maybe half a second before I answer. Yes, I will. What time?"

He said, "Dawn. Meet you at the livery?"

I said, "Sounds good. Let me buy you a beer, C.W., seeing as I now got me a job. And here comes Curly. Good evening, Marshal."

Curly plopped in the chair and said, "Not so much."

I was pouring him some beer. I stopped. "Not so much what?"

He said, "It ain't a good evening, and I ain't the marshal no more."

Knowlton nodded. I said, "Do what?"

Curly took a good swallow, wiped his moustache on his sleeve, and said, "The leaders of our fine town wont too happy with my fifteen-day shopping trip. For fresh whores."

I was pretty hot. "It ain't like they don't use 'em."

Curly said, "True enough. Soon as they fired me, they asked how the new ones looked. Whole durn council is probably over there right now to have a taste." He dug into his steak.

"Well," I said, "It don't matter. I got us a job with C.W. here. Riding guard for a week or so."

Knowlton said, "Hold on, now, Brodie, I can't afford both of you."

I said, "Won't cost you nothing more. I'll split my pay with him. It'll be twelve dollars each, Curly, to Tascosa and back."

Knowlton was waving both hands. "Brodie, we never got to talk about pay. This ain't as far as Dodge. I was thinking twenty dollars."

"If it was Dodge, it'd be fifty. I ain't ever been to Dodge with you. You paid me twenty-five for the Fort Supply trip. Tascosa ain't no closer than that. You have pissed me off, C.W. You pay us each fifteen or we ain't going."

Knowlton said, "But you said twelve."

Curly kicked me under the table.

"All right, twelve. But you feed us."

Knowlton stuck his hand out. "Deal. See y'all at dawn. And call me Punch."

As Knowlton walked out, I studied him. Slope-shouldered, going bald, maybe thirty or thirty-five, arms down near to his knees, flat nosed. Well over two hundred pounds. Not overly tall.

"What in Pete's name does Godiva see in him?" I wondered out loud.

Curly finished his beans and pushed back. "Lemme see. I'd say a big, good-natured white monkey. With money. What kind of a name is Punch?"

I said, "Durn if I know. Ain't that a simple tool for working leather?"

Curly laughed. "Sort of like him, I guess. Selling hides, harnesses, and such."

I stood up. "I'm off to get some sleep, 'cause in the morning I'm off to see my own true love."

In the morning we'd learn what Punch stood for. And that visit to Emmalee Byden? Well, maybe not.

Chapter Thirty-Seven

It being early spring, dawn was still late, and cool. With the wind it was cold.

I was near giddy. Cold water on my face and wrists, followed by a cold cloth bath. A slug of rum to swish around and spit into the basin before dumping it out the window.

Shirt next, then claw. Fresh socks, which my claw was special hard on, then trousers and boots and spurs. Shotgun chaps, against the thorns and wind, then into my suspenders and gun harness. Tied on my kerchief, which had a few claw holes too. Pulled on my Emmalee coat and jammed my hat on good against the wind. Pommel holsters over my left shoulder, bedroll over my left arm.

Checked the Winchester. Round in the chamber, half-cock.

Out the door, ready to ride. I tapped on Curly's door, but he was already gone. Still pretty spry for an old man.

Curly was all saddled and lashed down at the livery.

"Glad you could join us this fine afternoon," he said. It was still dark out.

"I believe you like this piebald," he went on. He put the blanket on, then helped me with the sadde and bedroll. He set up my pommel guns while I dropped the carbine in its scabbard.

Knowlton's men were dragging about, harnessing mules and putting some bows and canvas on the wagon loaded with goods.

Knowlton saw us then and walked into the stable, saying, "Good morning!" Always cheerful.

One of his shotgun riders followed him in, tapped on his shoulder, and said, "We need to talk, Knowlton."

Knowlton said, "Sure, Jarret. What about?"

"I heard what you're paying them two there, for riding guard. I'll take the same, or I ain't going."

"And you tell me this as we're leaving?"

Jarret grinned. "Figgered it's a good time for negotiating."

Knowlton's right fist came from down around his knee and slammed into Jarret's face like a steam piston. I think he left the ground. He wound up a couple of feet away, spread-eagled on his back, lights out. Nose clearly busted.

Punch, I thought. I looked at Curly and he nodded.

Knowlton rubbed his fist and said, "Y'all two mebbe go get some coffee. I got to find another shotgun rider. One who'll appreciate eight dollars."

We filled our canteens at the pump and headed back to the boardinghouse. This late, they'd have cook fires going. And coffee.

Knowlton joined us a half-hour later and took a mug of coffee.

"I hate a late start," he said. "But the coffee is good. Y'all ready?"

We set out due west. Straight behind us, the sun wont even up one finger.

We had tied off our spares behind a wagon, so me and Curly were free to range out and ahead of the wagons. I angled left.

Midmorning there was a gunshot from the wagons so we loped back to them.

As we pulled up, Curly said, "What's up?"

Knowlton pointed to a scrawny teenager watering a lathered horse.

The boy smiled. "Hey, y'all. Miz Turner sent me. Said she could use your help." It was Squeak, from the LT spread. He looked played out and his horse was worse.

Curly said, "You rode here, over a hundred miles, and didn't bring a spare?"

Squeak said, "I did, Marshal. Left him by the trail, maybe thirty mile shy of Mobeetie. Might be he lived."

"What is so all-fired pressing, boy?"

"Dadblame band of raiders is stealing us blind. Took over two hundred head before I left. Shot up some of the boys. Kilt two. Colonel Turner won't let us go after 'em. Says they got us outnumbered and we got to defend the headquarters."

Curly said, "You buy that?"

"Oh, heck no, Marshal. They's maybe eight, ten of 'em, but some of 'em is killers. We has as many as they do, but I don't think none of our buckaroos has been shot at before last week."

Curly turned to Knowlton. "Punch, I'm right sorry, but I made a pledge to this woman when her husband got sick. I got to go. Brodie, I know you want to go see that woman. No need for you to go with us. Brodie? Where in hell did he go?"

I said, "I'm back here putting Squeak's saddle on my spare. We'll trail his. And you know durn well I'm going with you."

Knowlton said, "Cookie, round 'em up a sack of grub." He stepped down off the wagon, went behind it, and untied his own horse. "Take him as a spare. Y'all look to be going hard at it from here. I can't pay you for no half day, but you're welcome to the grub. I'll get straight with you on the horse once we're all back in Mobeetie."

Not twenty minutes after that boy caught up to us, we was riding southeast.

We paced ourselves like we were Rangering, chasing bandits. Lope a while, walk a while.

Squeak said, "I think I loped the whole way here. Made it in two and a half days."

Curly said, "Yeah, and maybe killed a horse. Do you need to stop and sleep?"

"Nossir, Marshal. I sleep right good when we're walking 'em. Y'all make sure I wake up before y'all go to running again."

He was a tough kid. You had to like him.

After it got dark, Curly would only walk the horses and then only for an hour or two.

"We don't need to break no legs in no chuck holes, and we do need to be ready every day. Heck, we're liable to run into them scoundrels pushing LT cattle north."

Over jerky and corn dodgers the first night, Curly said, "Tell me about the rustlers. They Mex? Breeds?"

Squeak said, "They's some Texians with 'em, some breeds, but most is said to be white."

"Who says?"

"The boys that seen 'em. And didn't get kilt."

The second night we had a fire and beans and bacon. Curly said, "I can't for the life of me understand Lew Turner not going after them boys. You can't sit by and let folks run over you. You kill their leader and they're finished. Let's get some sleep."

Third night, we ate beans. The rest of the grub was gone. Curly said, "Didn't none of you go out and try a rifle shot at the bandito leader?"

"Marshal," Squeak said, "I done told you the Colonel is dug in. Won't let nobody do nothing but walk guard around his hacienda. It was Miz Turner as told me to slip away and come after you. I had tole her, I said, Miz Turner, that preacher figgers out we's dug in here, we'll be lucky if he don't come after us. That's when she . . ."

Curly blew up. "The preacher? The durn preacher is leading

'em? Why ain't you told me before?"

"You ain't asked, Marshal. I ain't no mind reader."

Despite Curly's concern about us being fresh and rested, he got us up long before daylight. I don't think he slept at all. I didn't much. At the crack of dawn we were riding hard. We got to the ranch at midmorning. Or close, anyways. The gunfire stopped us.

CHAPTER THIRTY-EIGHT

"Could that be coming from the ranch, Squeak?"

"Still a good ways off, Marshal, but I believe it is."

Curly said, "How far?"

"Mile, maybe. Cross that creek, up that little ridge, past that stand of trees, you're maybe a hundred fifty yards from the barn and bunkhouse. Hacienda is maybe fifty yards past them." Squeak unshucked his carbine, an old Spencer.

"Let's get in them trees. That's a lot of shooting. Ranch must be under attack." Curly pulled his big Winchester as he spoke.

I said, "Leave the spares here, Curly?" I don't know why I asked. He was already pulling his other mount toward the creek.

"We'll bring 'em," he said over his shoulder. "Might lose one or two in the fight and need to haul butt outta them trees. Don't dally, dammit."

Squeak and me chased him into those trees.

We tied off the horses in the near side of the woods and scooted through to the far side. It was laid out like Squeak had told us.

The gunfire was a steady banging, carbines and rifles mainly, but some pistol fire. I could see maybe six or seven men firing on the main house from behind the bunkhouse, barn, and horse shed. Must of been two or three more up in the barn loft.

We were looking at a front corner of the big house, with porches on both the side and front.

Gunsmoke was hanging over the whole durn place like a cloud.

"Where are their dadgum horses?" I said.

Curly pointed. "They's a few of 'em tied in the woods off to our right. You make 'em out? Maybe forty yards?"

I said, "Now I do."

Curly said, "Get over there, Brodie. When I open up, some of them yahoos is gonna run for their mounts. Let 'em get well in the open before you cut down on 'em. If anybody spots the preacher, focus on him. Squeak, let's blister them. Start slow. All this gunfire, they likely won't know we're here behind 'em 'til we kill a few."

And ker-blam, he lit in on them. I took off through the scrub for the bandits' ponies. As I got close, I realized there was somebody amongst their horses shooting at the house too. Horse guard.

I got pretty close and shot him in the back of the head, then took his place. He had a '66 rifle. I pulled some cartridges off his belt and topped off his rifle, then stuck his revolver in my belt. And got my breathing down to near normal.

By then Curly and Squeak had knocked down two of the bandits, and three was running toward me. One was limping bad. I saved him for last. He was hollering the whole way, "Dang it, Jack, quit shooting. It's me!"

When those three was down, I laid down my carbine and picked up that dead boy's rifle and put a few into the side of the barn, up high. Then the side door of the bunkhouse popped open and three more ran out, two to the barn and one toward me.

I focused on them two heading for the barn, for all the good that did. Got off six shots, kicked up dirt all around them, but didn't drop a one. I was shooting from behind a tree by then, as somebody in the main house had spotted my smoke and was shooting at me. Must have been a cowpoke, 'cause his shots wont even close.

That third man was halfway up the hill to me when I fired on him, and I heard a double boom from my partners off to my left. My shot stood him up, and the other two knocked him for a durn flip. They was both throwing three-hundred-fifty grain slugs, which will poleaxe a horse.

Squeak yelled at the house. "Hey, y'all, we're up in the trees. The banditos is in the barn." He was high-pitched, but it carried good. I didn't get no more incoming fire from the house.

About then another rustler broke from behind a rain barrel in back of the bunkhouse, crawling and scrambling to the barn. All of us shot at him. Nobody hit him but he was pretty well hid behind gunsmoke and dirt flying up around him. Heck, the house was firing on him too. I bet his clothes was shot to rags.

He wont in that barn two minutes before the back door flew open and five of them come pouring out on horseback, riding for the woods a hundred yards to my right and downhill.

It was a short ride. Four of them made it and kept going. Curly knocked down one horse, and the rider scrambled to the woods.

I heard Curly yelling, "Go get him, Brodie," but I was already moving.

Forty yards downhill, the bandit limped out into an opening, looked up, and said, "Jesus, Jack, you didn't bring us horses?"

Jack must of looked something like me, before I shot him. I remember we both had gray hats. I shot this one and said, "I ain't Jack." He started crawling away so I nailed him down with a second shot.

As I eased up to him, he twitched so I put a third one in him. Curly and Squeak came crashing down through the scrub about then.

Curly said, "You got him?"

I said, "I did." I was still breathing hard.

He said, "You get a look at them others?"

I said, "Preacher Vance was the second rider out the door. He was exactly like Billy drew him."

"Durn it to hell," Curly said. "I thought so too. We must of killed six or seven of 'em, and missed him."

Miz Turner's big foreman Hernando eased onto the hacienda porch with a long-barrelled shotgun. Squeak yelled at him, "Could be one or two left in the barn. We'll check the bunk-house."

We went down and did that, after checking the bodies on the hill and behind the buildings. Hernando had six of his men surround the barn, and then he ducked in alone.

There were two shotgun blasts and he came out. "Clear," he said. "Only one."

Curly said, "Where's Lew?"

Hernando nodded toward the main house. "In bed," he said. "Not so good."

Curly said, "You follow 'em, and they might lead you to your rustled cattle. I'm gonna be after 'em soon as I check on Miz Turner."

Hernando said, "I will take five men and go. Squeak, you and Valdez, you help us get saddled, then wait with the *Jefe* and *Señora* Turner. I think they maybe put them cattle in Bull Canyon, down by the Rio Pease."

Once Hernando and his men rode off, Squeak and me brought our horses down and watered and fed them and changed saddles. Curly went on in the big house.

As we pulled our mounts up to the rail alongside the porch, Curly and Miz Turner stepped outside. She smiled and waved to me and Squeak, but kept talking to Curly. Her face was cut and there was blood on her white shirt. I thought she looked pretty good to have gone through a durn gunfight and had all her windows shot out.

I couldn't make out their talk until Curly said, "Yessum. Yessum, don't you worry. Me and Brodie mean to track 'em and kill 'em, every dang one."

He nodded goodbye and jammed on his hat. I think she squeezed his arm. He come off that porch and in three strides he was in the saddle and heading south, jerking his spare behind him. Over his shoulder, he said, "Thankee, Squeak. Brodie, don't dally. Try and keep up."

I did.

Twenty minutes south, Preacher's tracks turned west. Hernando's posse had kept going south.

"I didn't think Preacher would go back to his rustled herd. He ain't got the men to move 'em, and he's got to think them cowpokes will be more worried about getting back them cows than chasing bandits."

"Well," I said, "it appears old Preacher was right."

"I don't blame Hernando none. His job is the herd and the ranch," Curly said. "The preacher couldn't of seen you back there. He'll head for them new ranches around Tascosa. See how he's already angling to the northwest? His problem is he don't know we're back here."

"Our problem is there's at least four of them and two of us."

He said, "That ain't a problem. We can take 'em like we took 'em back at the ranch, long as we don't let 'em ambush us."

"Well, then, Curly, I guess we got it made. Ain't but maybe a thousand ambush sites 'twixt here and Tascosa."

He snorted. "There you go again, missing the good side. Think on it like that little gambler back in Dodge City. We got more targets than them."

CHAPTER THIRTY-NINE

"It ain't but the four of 'em," Curly said. "Got no pack horse nor spares. You can see they're riding hard. Mebbe they do think they're being chased. Anyways, they're pulling away 'cause we have to track 'em, and we got to watch for ambushes."

"Yeah," I said. "And pull these durn spares."

He said, "These extry ponies will be the difference in our favor, in the long run. They can't afford one to pull up lame. They got to pace themselves. Once they figger that out, they'll slow down. And we'll catch up to 'em."

"Ain't that when they'll look to ambush us, Marshal?"

"Well, yes, I believe you're right. So, long as they keep kicking up dirt we'll push on, but soon as we see they've come down to a walk, we'll grow cautious. Another thing. They ain't provisioned up like us, neither."

I said, "Seems like another good reason for 'em to turn back on us."

"Well," he said, "there is that."

Wasn't long before they slowed down and so did we.

Their trail led into a rocky dry creek bed. Pretty deep. Full of slate, caves, and mesquite. Looked scary as Hell to me.

Curly said, "It's a lot like Bull Canyon, back there near the LT spread."

I said, "We gonna follow 'em into that?"

"Oh, heck no, Brodie. You crazy? Shoot, it's as good a ambush site as you could wish for."

"So?"

"We'll ride the north rim. Keep an eye down in there for 'em."

I said, "All right, but what if they leave out over the south rim?"

"Hmmm," he said. "I take your point. Tell you what. We'll split up. You ride the south side, I'll take this one. It don't look to get more'n two, three hundred yards wide. We'll figger out where to hook back up once things flatten out again."

Me and my big mouth. Now here we was, chasing four killers, and us split up.

I dallied the rope from my spare pony around my fancy nickel saddle horn and drew my carbine.

A mile down the wash, Curly signaled me to come over to his side. They had turned north.

We were too tired to talk that night. Curly laid our lariats out in a circle around us like always, we ate some jerky and dodgers, and I was out cold about two seconds after my head hit the saddle.

It was a cold night. Come dawn, I surely admired that coat Emmalee had made me. We brewed a pot of coffee while we saddled up, drank a cup standing, and then hit the trail before it was full light.

"What happened back there, Curly?'

"At the ranch?"

"Yeah. At the ranch. Where in heck was Lew Turner?"

"In bed, like Hernando said. Wouldn't let nobody ride out and attack the bandits. Probably would of caught 'em all split up, what with them out rounding up batches of cattle from here and yonder. Preacher and his boys rode in there not even an hour before us. Killed one ranch hand down by the barn, bad wounded another, then commenced to shooting up the hacienda."

I said, "And then we showed up. Behind 'em."

"Yep." Curly said. "Miz Turner said it was right 'fortuitious.' I told her I wasn't too familiar with that word."

"Me neither. Not that particular word, anyways."

"Brodie, she said I had 'good timing.' Couldn't of come at a better time, unless it was sooner, which of course it couldn't be. She squeezed my arm when she said it."

"I have seen her do that, Curly. How did she take the colonel laying in bed through all this?"

"I don't think she was pleased totally. Said that in the middle of the shooting, afore we broke in, he tried to get up. Said he would cut a deal with 'em."

I said, "What stopped him?"

Curly shrugged. "She already had her face cut from flying glass. He took one look at her and said, 'Oh, my God!' And fell on the floor holding his chest like he'd been shot, but he weren't. Mostly he sat the whole thing out, telling folks what to do. He ain't changed much, in fifteen years."

I thought, maybe old Curly's timing ain't bad at all. I believe that thought evaded him completely.

What he said was, "These boys is smart. They's looking to follow the Prairie Dog Town Fork up to the short crossing of the Llano, probably pick up the Canadian and make for Las Vegas or Santa Fe." He wont thinking about no Miz Turner, that much was clear. Stone lawman, through and through.

I said, "Don't that mean they could duck into the Palo Duro, or maybe head to Tascosa?"

"They could. They surely could. Now, I don't want to track them into no Palo Duro Canyon. No, sir. Tell you what. They go in that canyon? We'll skirt it and go wait at Tascosa. See where they pop up next."

I said, "Well, the word gets out I'm in Tascosa, I believe Preacher will come. He means to kill me 'less I kill him first."

"Yeah, you're probably right. And I think he may feel honor-bound to retake them women too." He sat straight up in the saddle and said, "Heads up. Ain't that a horse in that draw up on the right? You see him?"

"I do," I said. "He crippled or hobbled? Look how he's limping."

"Dismount," Curly said. "That horse is still saddled. We'll tie off and go up afoot."

We drew long guns and did that. The horse wasn't hobbled. It was full lame. Pitiful.

"They ain't no kind of men," I said. "Leaving it like that. Why didn't they shoot it? They got enough of a lead on us, we wouldn't of heard it. Not down in these breaks."

"They don't know that," he said. He looked around. "Or maybe they do. Get back to the horses, Brodie. Quick. They may be after our mounts!"

We scrambled and was halfway back and starting to feel foolish when a bullet spanged off a rock beside Curly and peppered him with splinters. A couple more shots zinged overhead before I spotted their smoke above another gully maybe forty yards away.

We both threw some rounds at the smoke but then Curly yelled, "Behind us."

Two riders busted out of a wash and went straight for our horses, firing pistols at us as they rode.

Curly shot one out of his saddle. I think I winged the other one. I saw dust fly off his leg, maybe, but there was so much smoke, and us bobbing and weaving and him juking through the brush that he made it. He untied my spare pony, and beat it for the gully where their shooters were.

"Kill 'em!" Curly screamed. A big man in a sombrero stood

up in the gully to grab my spare. Curly nailed him and he went down as I put two rounds in the pony.

Quick as that, it was over. We could hear riders clattering away on that shale.

Well, it was almost over.

We went to check the near one, the first one Curly shot, and he wont finished. Fired a shot as we crept close, but he was shooting at noise.

Curly yelled at him, "Fire again and I will leave you for the critters. I know you're hurt bad. I dusted you on both sides. Your partners have rid off. Toss that pistol toward us."

There was another shot but it wasn't at us. That bandit took the fast way out. His horse had bolted and was probably halfway back to the LT spread by then.

Over in the far gully in the ambush site we found my spare pony struggling to stay upright, and a big Mex on his back gurgling and blinking. I put the pony down. The gunshot caused the Mex to flinch.

Curly said, "You must be Chico. Preacher and your other *companero* has left you. Was Preacher hit any?"

Chico had blood coming from his mouth, and as he blinked his eyes flicked right and left. Like he was looking for a way out.

"No way out of this one," Curly said. "I see you're in no mood to talk. I'll say goodbye."

Curly drew his revolver to finish the man, but a bullet had hit it and sprung the cylinder.

"Durn," he said. "Tore my holster too. A pure wonder it didn't break my hip. Brodie, will you finish this one? I hate to waste a rifle cartridge on a dying man."

I shot Chico, and we got moving again. Minus one horse. We didn't bury none of them, but we did put down that lame horse they'd set the trap with.

CHAPTER FORTY

Some miles shy of the Palo Duro canyon we spied some riders crossing our path heading east. Curly got his glass on them, then passed it to me.

"Two horses, bearing three riders? That how you see 'em?"

"Yep," I said. "And cowpunchers. Not our banditos."

We hailed them and hooked up pretty quick.

"Yessir, Marshal, we know of your Preacher. Hank here ran into 'em heading out to ride the line. Took his horses, guns, water, and grub. Pure luck we found him before he perished." The oldest one did the talking, mostly. "I'm hoping the foreman will let me take some boys and go after 'em."

Hank said, "Don't know why they didn't shoot me."

Curly said, "They was likely worried we might hear the gunfire. I'm surprised they didn't stab you, though."

"I believe they was studying on it. One was shot up some. High on his right leg. When the other one started to dismount, I took off running."

I said, "The preacher wont wounded?"

"Not so far as I could tell. That long black coat, maybe so, but he didn't act hurt none."

The older cowpoke said, "Hank says when they first come up on him they asked did he know of a doctor. Ain't that right, Hank?"

"It is," Hank said. "I tole 'em weren't no real doctors nowhere near, 'cept maybe that sheep doctor up to Tascosa."

The older man said, "That old sumbitch is so ill-natured I don't think I'd want him cutting on me if my leg was a-falling off."

"Byden," I said.

"Yessir, that's him. Ill-natured sumbitch."

Curly said, "So, they's heading for Tascosa?"

Hank said, "You'd think so, one of 'em hurt and all. Surely where I'd go. Rather have a ill-natured sumbitch cut on me than nobody at all. Still, durn if they didn't head like they was going into the canyon. You ain't gonna chase 'em in there, is you?"

"Nope," said Curly. "Place is too hairy. We'll go on to Tascosa and lay in wait there. How far you got to go?"

"Camp's maybe fifteen, eighteen miles."

Curly said, "You better take our spare. This is awful rough country for riding double."

The old one said, "Can't pay you much. I ain't got three dollars, all told. Hank, you got any?"

"That preacher made me turn out my pockets."

Curly said, "We need to move. Tell your foreman to get the horse back to me in Tascosa. Or leave it in Mobeetie, if somebody goes there first."

It was late in the day when we rode into Tascosa. Durn if it hadn't grown some more. We headed straight to Kendall's blacksmith shop and house. As we passed near I couldn't help but stare at Emmalee's place. I was hoping to catch a glimpse at least, even though it was probably too cool to have a baby outside.

Curly caught me looking.

"Don't even think about it," he said.

"About what?"

"Going there. We don't need you and Rawley Byden crossways

while we's trying to get set for that durn Preacher."

I said, "But, ain't we got to warn them? Ain't Byden the bait?"

Curly pulled his hat and scratched his scalp. "Yeah, but . . ."

"But, hell, Curly. We got to get her out of there. Preacher knows her. He ain't ever seen Byden, but he knows Emmalee. Probably means to find her while he's here. We got to hide her."

"You're right, Brodie. You're exactly right. We'll get Kendall and Billy to watch her and the baby. I mean, if Byden goes along with it."

"If he don't, Curly, I'll by God take 'em. I ain't leaving them there as part of no trap."

"All right, Brodie, calm down. We'll talk to Kendall. Maybe him and his missus can swing it without Byden knowing you're even here. I don't think he's gonna let her go to be nowhere near you, baby or not."

"Shoot. I hadn't thought on it that way."

He said, "No, you ain't. You're thinking, 'Here I come to save my lady,' and I'm trying to get you to remember we are here to kill Preacher. All right? Him, and anybody with him. Your lady will be pretty durn proud of you if we do this. And if we don't, she's probaby ruint."

"All right. All right, Curly, I got it. Where we gonna stay?"

"We'll ask Kendall."

Kendall's cabin was like Old Home Day, leastways at first. Billy and Conchita jumping around like the teenagers they were, Miz Terrazas jabbering Mex, mostly, and Kendall talking over them like he was used to it. I noticed Billy was talking better.

Curly gave them a short version of what we'd been up to and what we expected, but when I asked about Emmalee and what kind of baby she had, things went dark. And quiet.

Kendall finally said, "What she had was a dead one. It come

way too early, a month or more, and the cord went around her
neck. Little girl. The missus helped with it is how I know.
Dadgum Byden ain't had squat to say about it. And we don't
hardly even see Miz Byden no more."

Losing a baby wont no rare thing on the frontier. Probably
true most anywheres back then, but there was something else
hanging in the air. Something unsaid as yet.

My head was about to explode.

I said, "What ain't you telling us?"

Kendall hung his head a second, then said, "Tell you what.
Us fellers will go over to the Black Cat, the saloon, get us a
drink. I'll tell you all I know. Y'all got to go there anyways."

Curly said, "We do?"

"Unless you wish to sleep on my floor. They's rooms to let
over there, with or without a working girl."

"Good," Curly said. "We'll drop our traps, hear you out, then
figger out where to wait."

I said, "And how to get Emmalee out of there and put up
safe. Durn Preacher could be here tomorrow or the next day."

I was wrong.

CHAPTER FORTY-ONE

Billy and Conchita took care of our horses. Curly and me got a room and dropped off our bedrolls and saddle guns, then met Kendall in the saloon.

"Well?" I said. I was fit to be tied.

"Well, I heard y'all talk before, you and the marshal here. I know you got feelings for Miz Emmalee. Still, I don't want to say nothing that'll cause you to do something you'll regret."

"Dammit, Kendall, you ain't my momma. You ain't even Curly. How about don't worry none about my regrets and tell me what's going on. Is she all right?"

"Far as I can tell, Brodie, her health is fine now. My missus has maybe seen some bruises, but Emmalee coulda fell."

I stood up. "You buy that?"

Curly said, "Easy, Brodie. She's Byden's wife. This is touchy ground."

"Byden's the one on touchy ground," I near shouted. "I'll kill him."

Kendall said, "See now? That's what I was afeared of. Lookie here, Brodie. You can beat his sorry butt to a frazzle and won't nobody raise an eyebrow. Do I think she fell? Maybe, but if she did, it was his doing. That sweet young thing, and crotchety miserable old . . . But you can't walk in there and shoot him."

I said, "You still ain't said what you know."

Kendall's head drooped. "Bottom line? Billy and Conchita heard 'em fighting, the night she lost the baby. I think Byden tussled with her, maybe hit her. And that's why it come early. The young'uns were taking food over from the missus and they heard it all. He was cussing and she was crying, and they heard a thump and her scream, so they come got us."

I was pulling on my coat when Curly said, "You hold it right there. We got other fish to fry. You can settle up with him when this is over, but I need him setting in that cabin as bait. And you and Kendall need to figger out how to get her outta there without Byden knowing you got anything to do with it."

I was about beyond reason. Might have ruined my friendship with Curly right then, spoiled his vengeance on the preacher, if it wasn't for a drunk cowpoke.

He staggered in off the street and said, "Don't nobody get beat up or shot for a hour or two. All right? Y'all hear me?"

The bartender said, "Why's that, Toby?"

"That old sheep doctor has got his hands full, that's why come. Some preacher took a gunshot case in there. I steered 'em to him. Dang, it's cold out there."

"Well, now," Curly said. "Don't that change everything."

He wasn't asking.

What we settled on was to send Billy with some food to make sure it was really our Preacher, and to get a feel for the inside of Byden's cabin. Billy had growed up so much since Preacher killed his momma that it was hardly no way Preacher would tie him to that Alley Cat whorehouse in Mobeetie, so many months ago. We had Billy take a note, writ by Kendall, asking Miz Byden to come see Kendall's wife right away if she could.

That was Curly's idea, on the outside chance Preacher didn't recognize Emmalee neither. If we got her out of there we could burn the durn cabin down on them, including Byden for all I cared. But I wasn't a total fool.

"Good luck with that, Curly."

"I know, Brodie. I feel the same, but we got to try. I'll be right outside the door. If she comes out with Billy, or if the preacher steps into sight, I'll kill him."

"Yeah, but it ain't likely. You got that little Remington two-shooter?"

Curly said, "I do. Why?"

"Well, if your plan don't work, I'll stick that derringer inside my can and go in as a hostage. Trade me for Emmalee. I'm who he wants."

Kendall said, "Your can?"

"The can that fits on my left wrist. Holds the claw. You seen it."

Curly said, "Preacher will kill you the second he sees you. We don't gain nothing."

"He won't see me until Emmalee is clear. That's the deal. Once I'm inside, you fire on the cabin. Distract 'em. I'll try to get 'em with the derringer."

Curly said, "I don't like it. Durn derringer ain't much against two men."

Kendall said, "I got a little six-shot Smith and Wesson. Thirty-two pocket gun, cut down. Ought to fit in your boot."

"They'll search him," Curly said. "Find that right off."

"Good," I said. "They find one, they'll quit looking. I know it ain't too great a plan, Curly. What's yours?"

"I got nothing better, Brodie. Here's the derringer. Give him yours too, Kendall. Let's try this. Billy, you ready?"

Billy was in and out in no time. Emmalee didn't come with him.

I said, "Did he know you?"

"Nossir, Brodie. But it's him."

Curly said, "Are the Bydens tied up?"

Billy shook his head. "Byden's working. Doctorin'."

"Preacher ask for anything? Fresh horses?"

Billy shook his head again.

"Well," Curly said, "That ain't good."

Kendall said, "How come?"

"Means they ain't studying leaving. They're waiting for Brodie, right here. They don't know he's already in town."

"All right," I said. "Time for me to go in. Curly, I'm gonna tell 'em they got you back when they made that stab at our horses. You stay out of sight and if this goes bad, you kill 'em when they come out. Billy and Kendall can help you."

"We might hit Emmalee."

"That's better'n her being left with 'em. But be durn sure you do accidental hit Byden." I left my nice coat off so's I could maybe get to that gun.

I walked out. Durn if it didn't start to rain. Ain't that the way things go.

Chapter Forty-Two

I stood clear of the door and yelled, "Hello, Preacher Vance. I hear you're looking for me."

There was a rush of muttering inside. Byden said, "Who's there?"

"It's me, Byden. Brodie Dent. And I know Preacher's got you. He ain't hurt Emmalee, has he?"

More muttering inside. I was freezing.

"He ain't hurt us yet. I tole him who you are. He wants you."

I said, "He can't talk?"

"I can talk. You worried about Miss Emmalee here? Is that what I hear?"

After all this time I got to hear his voice. Figured it would be deep and rich like the chaplain at Fort Elliott. It was high pitched. Right squeaky.

"You don't sound like no preacher. Sound right squeaky, I'd say. Lemme talk to the preacher."

I was hoping he'd get pissed off and come out shooting. Curly was at the other corner of the cabin. He'd of cut the preacher in half. No such luck.

"I'm Preacher Vance, and I ain't alone. Where's that other lawman was with you? Tell him to show himself."

I said, "You'll see him in Hell soon enough. Y'all killed him when you tried for our horses."

"You and me are gonna talk," he screamed. "Sooner than later. You want this woman? Come and save her. Come on in.

196

Me and Pecker Johnson is fixing to have a go at her. Or you can stay out there and listen."

I said, "She didn't kill your stuttering idjit brother. I did. I'll trade me for her. Let her go and I'll walk right in."

"You don't want the Doc?"

"I don't care what you do with him," I yelled back. "Better keep him. You might need him after we fight."

"You ain't getting the woman first. You'll take her and run. Nossir. You come on in, then she can leave."

There it was. He was right. I had to go in.

I pushed and the door swung in. It was a one-room place. Emmalee was sitting on the floor by the bed and the second bandit was laying on it, bandaged leg and all. Byden stood against the back wall.

Emmalee looked right scared, which come as no surprise. I smiled at her and stepped inside. It was toasty warm and felt good for a second. Then Preacher hit me.

He come from behind the door and butt-stroked me in the side of my head with his carbine. I think Emmalee screamed, but I went down and was in and out for some minutes. I heard the door slam and heard Preacher say, "Is that him?"

Byden said, "It's him. Look at his claw. You gonna let us go now?"

"I never made no deal about you, Doc, but it don't matter. She ain't going nowhere, either."

I figured as much, but Byden wouldn't give up.

"But you said you'd trade. Go on and kill him and let us go. You got what you came for."

Preacher said, "You want me to kill him? So he's a problem for you?"

Byden snorted. "He ain't no better than you. Been after my wife ever since he killed your brother."

"Well, you'll get to watch him die real slow. Stick that poker down in the grate. I want it white hot. Get up and search him, Pecker."

"Boss, my leg is killing me. We ain't getting ready to run again, is we?"

"I'm leaving and taking these two as hostages. You can come or stay here and hang. First I'm gonna burn that one-armed booger to death, one stroke at a time."

Pecker found Kendall's pistol right away. While he was checking my legs I palmed that derringer. Moaned a little to cover my movement.

"He's clean, Boss. Can I lay down now?"

"Hold my carbine on 'em, and hand me that poker. Watch this, Doc."

I was still on my stomach and pretending to be out cold. I don't know why, but I figured he'd burn my back first. No sir. He went right for the jewels. I felt the heat on the back of my thighs before he touched me, and realized where he was heading with that hot iron.

I poked my butt up and got it burned good. Flipped over, swatted the hot poker away with my can, then grabbed it with my claw. Put a fat little forty-one-caliber slug right in Preacher's brisket. He fell back some but kept his feet under him. He coughed and stared at that hole in his middle for a second then pulled his pistol. It went off while he was drawing it but didn't hit nothing.

Emmalee screamed, and poor old Pecker turned to look at her. I sat up and shot him too. He went down.

I dropped the empty derringer and took the cold end of the poker in my good hand. That was a good thing. It had already about ruint what was left of my left palm and thumb. Could be I screamed too.

I bounced up pretty good, considering. I jabbed Preacher, and caused him to miss with his next shot, then whacked him with the hot end. He tried to block it with his pistol and it went off again, right by my head. He stepped back out of my reach as I got dizzy.

Funny thing, right then. I had this thought. Brodie, I thought, you did all right there, up to a point.

I heard him cock it again and braced for the shot. The blast caused me to flinch, but the window exploded in and Preacher's head exploded too. A .45-75 will do that. Good old Sally Ann had claimed another man.

It was all over so fast. I picked up Preacher's Colt and stuck it in my trousers front before I noticed my left sleeve was afire. That durn hot poker.

The door got kicked in, and here come Curly. "Did I hit him? Did I get him? Them windows ain't clear." He was dripping wet.

Emmalee dragged me to the pump, got it going, and put out my shirt-sleeve fire.

And I hugged her. "You all right, Baby? They didn't hurt you?" Can't believe I called her "Baby."

Curly said, "I told you it was a good plan, Brodie. I'm glad you didn't mess it up."

Rawley Byden said, "Get your hands off my wife, Dent, you little buffalo turd."

I looked over Emmalee's head and there he was, pointing Pecker's big Remington at me.

And I had thought it was over.

Everybody heard him cock it.

Emmalee pushed away from me, backing toward him. "You are not the man I married, Rawley Byden. Much as I hate you, I cannot believe you could do this. He has saved me twice."

She faced him, hands behind her. She kept shifting, keeping herself between me and him.

In a low spitting voice, she said, "What will you do with his body, Rawley? Hide it out on the prairie, like you did with my little girl?"

Good Lord. I saw what she was doing. She had taken Preacher's pistol out of my trousers while she was up against me. He shoved her aside with one hand and said, "Stay out of this. I'll finish it here."

She shot him. He went white-faced and stumbled back. She shot him again.

I saw his lights go out as he fell backward and down.

I said, "Lord, woman, you shot him twice."

She tossed the pistol on his body. "I'd have shot him more but it went empty."

I touched his neck. "Your husband is dead, Emmalee."

"He hasn't been my husband since they first took me."

Curly, Kendall, and Billy helped me drag the three bodies outside, while Señora Terrazas and Conchita helped Emmalee clean up some.

Pretty soon Emmalee said, "It's late. Please put Rawley where the coyotes can't get him tonight, and we'll bury him and finish cleaning tomorrow. Brodie, you stay here. I want to watch that burnt hand. Take off that claw."

The others looked at each other, then scurried out. Emmalee took my burnt paw and kissed it, and then took my face and kissed me square on the mouth.

I said, "I ain't ever spent the evening with no lady."

She said, "Good."

It was the best night of my life. Up to that point, anyways.

CHAPTER FORTY-THREE

Clouds was nowhere to be seen, come morning. Talk about a bright new day. Cool, crisp, clear. Springtime, by goshen.

Curly swung by on his way out. Full packed, pulling a spare. He said, "I figgered there wasn't no way you'd be thinking of leaving this place soon. Maybe never, right? Kendall said to tell you they need some law here. Him and the store owner will put you up for it. Think on it. I mean, if you can find a place to stay, could be you're all set here. Fixed up." Big grin.

Emmalee came out and snuggled under my left arm, shivering like the dickens. She felt good there. It was almost enough to make me forget my burned left thumb.

"Marshal," she said. "Won't you dismount and come in? I've made coffee."

"Thank you, Miss Emmalee, but Kendall's missus done fed me like a king. I'll say so long. Pretty good ride ahead."

I said, "Back to Mobeetie?"

He grinned. "Maybe not. Might go south. Might know of a rich widder woman."

He wheeled away to start that long trek back to the LT spread. I squeezed Emmalee and said, "Talk about a 'Good Bad Man?' There goes one."

ABOUT THE AUTHOR

McKendree R. (Mike) Long III is a former soldier with two combat tours as an advisor to South Vietnamese Army units. His awards and decorations include the Silver Star, the Parachutist Badge, the Combat Infantryman's Badge, and the Vietnamese Cross of Gallantry (Gold and Silver Stars).

After retiring from the Army in 1980, he was a financial advisor with a major investment firm for twenty-nine years. He and his wife Mary have two married daughters, four grandchildren, and a great-grandson. He holds a BS in Business Administration, and is a gun enthusiast. He's a member of Western Writers of America, Western Fictioneers, Military Writers Society of America, and Ozark Creative Writers. He is often found on Seabrook Island, South Carolina.